MW00789659

Concert
at Chopin's House

a collection of Polish-American writing
edited by John Minczeski

Many Minnesotas Project Number 4

NEW RIVERS PRESS 1987

Copyright © 1987 by New Rivers Press, Inc.
ISBN 0-89823-098-5
Library of Congress Catalog Card Number: 87-62991
All rights reserved
Typesetting and Book Design: Peregrine Publications, Inc.
Photographs by Paul Petroff

Concert at Chopin's House has been published with the aid of grant support
from the Metropolitan Regional Arts Council (with funds appropriated by the
Minnesota State Legislature), the First Bank System Foundation, and the
National Endowment for the Arts (with funds appropriated by the Congress
of the United States).

New Rivers Press books are distributed by

The Talman Company	and	Bookslinger
150-5th Ave.		213 E. 4th St.
New York, NY		St. Paul, MN
10011		55101

Concert at Chopin's House has been manufactured in the United States of
America for New Rivers Press, Inc. (C. W. Truesdale, editor/publisher),
1602 Selby Ave., St. Paul, MN 55104 in a first edition of 2000 copies.

*For Stephanie, B. P., and those who
stayed behind in Poland.
For the living and the dead.*

Contents

Photographs by Paul Petroff

Frontispiece from Poland
Photographs on pp. 52-55 from Mexico
Photographs on pp. 76-79 from India
Photographs on pp. 114-117 from Peru
Photographs on pp. 134 137 from Seattle
Photograph on p. 201 from India

Introduction

T he writing in this anthology comes from everywhere — New York, Pennsylvania, California, Minnesota. The ancestors of these writers came from nowhere. That is to say, they were born in Poland in the 19th century when it had fallen off all the geo-political maps and become part of Russia, or Germany, or the Austro-Hungarian Empire. In the Age of Empire you simply could not be a world-class power without some territory to call your own. Poles started leaving what used to be Poland in record numbers. They didn't want to be drafted into German, Czarist or Hapsburg armies and be ordered to shoot fellow Poles involved in the latest insurrection.

My grandfather was one of them. Old Bronislaw had decided he would either attend the University or go to America. At the age of 18, with help from an aunt, he left Poland. The fact that he wasn't in line to inherit the small family farm made the decision to emigrate easier. My grandfather's story is not very unique. He arrived in this country in 1910 with a Russian passport and forged documents stating he was Russian Orthodox, was honorably discharged from the Russian Army and was 28 years old. A brief section of his passport indicates that he had paid a considerable sum for what amounted to an exit tax. Just off the boat, he wandered around New York in a state of confusion until somebody spotted him and took him to a policeman who spoke Polish.

That first day in New York, he saw a Black man crossing the street. The nuns used to tell stories about people who sold their souls to the devil and turned black at the moment they died. They also told stories about people receiving communion while in mortal sin, and choked on the host at the communion rail. Their faces turned black instantly, and they keeled over backwards, dead. I heard the stories from Polish nuns while I was growing up in South Bend, Indiana. My grandfather, who heard these stories in the village of Jelenie Gora near Białystok, never had an inkling that real Black people existed in this world. He thought he had just seen the devil incarnate.

Since there was no Poland on the map, he and others brought Poland with them. Brought it in their accents, in their cooking, their music, their stubborn ways. My mother, who is Pennsylvania Dutch, had to convert not only to Catholicism, but to Polishness as well. She pronounced Polish surnames with precision and confidence, cooked a mean kielbasa (hand-made by Clem at the College Locker Plant) but never tackled pierogi. That was for people like my grandmother who began her apprenticeship to Polish cooking at the age of three or four, like a violin virtuoso. She cooked and canned and brought forth feast after magnificent feast every Christmas and Easter, having spent weeks in preparation, consulting in Polish with green grocers and butchers and other grandmothers. This was not a perfect world, but that didn't mean we were going to accept second best where Christmas and Easter dinners were concerned. The vegetables came from old B. P. Minczewski's garden. He'd dug up half his back yard for the sake of tomatoes, peppers, beans, cauliflowers, carrots, cabbage. Every year his compost trench was in a different spot. It was a serious and tidy working garden. He rotated his small beet and sweet corn crops. And he kept it up to the end, this being on speaking terms with the earth.

Once, I was in 5th grade, I told my grandmother that I might like to write a couple of novels under a penname. Why, she asked. Wasn't I proud of my own name? I thought about it. No one wrote under a Polish name in this country. We were a country of Smiths and Joneses. Besides, the Poles had taken such a beating during the cruel era of the Polish joke that to admit you were actually Polish seemed tantamount to admitting you had a deep and severe character flaw. You wanted to go around apologizing for some stupidity you probably committed but were unaware of.

I wasn't the first in the family to consider changing his name. Poles were under a double burden when they arrived here. They came first of all from a country that existed only in its culture and language, and they had names no one could pronounce. So old B. P., when he sold insurance in Albany, New York, or Buffalo, had considered changing his name to something like McChesney or Manchester. Thanks to the Metropolitan Life Insurance Company, I ended up Minczeski and not McChesney— an Irishman without a portfolio. Metropolitan, on learning that he was moving to South Bend with my grandmother's family, talked him into keeping his Polish name. *Sell life insurance to the Polish of South Bend*. And he did. (I can imagine, though, the looks he would get if he introduced himself as "B. P. Manchester" in his thick accent that had Poland written all over it.)

My wife's father did change his name—from John Thomas Lewandowski to just John Thomas. His brothers and sisters were born in Poland, but he, the youngest, was born in this country. It wasn't until after I was married that I learned my wife was as Polish as I. She had "passed" in the dominant culture without the occasional ridicule of being Polish. The price for that was missing out on the rituals, feasts, and loud family gatherings that helped make being Polish in the middle of the North American continent easier to bear and even, occasionally, celebrated. The Z. B. Falcons (a Polish-American fraternal organization) held a gathering each year at a picnic grounds just outside the South Bend City limits. The Z. B. Falcon precision drill team marched and twirled flags on the parade field. Galvanized tubs full of dry ice and beer and pop were scattered in the shade, and there were political speeches that I couldn't understand because Polish wasn't spoken in our house. But they probably extolled the Polish heroes who helped make this country great—Kosciusko and Count Polaski— and bestowed their virtues on the guy running for prosecuting attorney.

Literature and a compelling sense of history (repelling attacks by the fierce Tatars and routing the Turks during the siege of Vienna in 1683) helped keep Polish cultural identity alive during foregin domination. But Polish history was generally unavailable to second and third generation Polish-Americans in the fifties and sixties, and Polish literature consisted of Joseph Conrad's novels and stories. "The Secret Sharer" is in practically every high school English Literature Anthology. We could take a measure of pride in Conrad, who remains one of this century's best writers in English. His incredibly sensitive and adept treatment of character and the dark side of the human psyche (Winnie Verlag, in *The Secret Agent*, for example) helped us ignore the cultural stereotype we were being forced into—not only by Polish jokes, but by examples in American fiction where we were often represented as loutish brutes.

Fortunately, there is now a growing list of contemporary Polish writers available in translation in the U.S.: Rożewicz, Szymborska, Herbert, Miłosz, Konwicki, Borowski, etc. These, along with other central and eastern European writers and poets are, like Conrad, of importance to all readers, not just those who claim a particular ethnic heritage.

The writers in this anthology, while they've successfully integrated into the melting pot, have gone a long way to keeping their ancestral roots and familial history alive. And they're maintaining a strong literary tradition while being part of the current boom in American writing. Most of the writers in this collection have some connection to the upper Midwest. But people drift away, they move back, or simply knock around inventing some migratory pattern as their grandparents might have done after they entered New York from Ellis Island. For the sake of eclecticism, I have included a writer or two with no ostensible connection to mid-continent America, and one writer who sent the following by way of a biography:

> Having taken my husband's name, religion, points of view and admirations, e.g., the shoulder line of Czeslaw Miłosz's jacket (cover *Ironwood 18*, '81) and the man in it, I now claim some of his heritage, lineage through marriage vows, and pass myself off as Polish, the pay off having these poems published. People like me are not to be trusted. How can my Polish (born Latvian) husband say he still loves me? His deep-set brown eyes, his chubby fingers still tender when they observe me. How is it? I have not taken *that* trait?—Perhaps my husband is used to a kind of Germanic fraudulence: *his* Polish father married a German, and now he has married one. Or maybe he hopes, because we've given up geographical separations, we are now, in this country, one.

Not one of the writers in this collection is a household word. We trust that situation will change over time. Certainly the quality of their writing speaks for itself.

I'd like to thank Bill Truesdale for dreaming up this project and for giving me the opportunity to spend time with these authors and their writing. He's also been of great assistance to me in editing this collection. A grant from the Metropolitan Regional Arts Commission (with funds appropriated by the Minnesota State Legislature) made the publication of this book possible.

John Minczeski
St. Paul, 1987

Concert at Chopin's House

Paul Milenski

Genesis

D uring boys' prayer Stanley Merski sat proud and erect, folded his hands on his desk, aimed his eyes straight ahead. All the other boys did the same, but Stanley knew he could sit with erect posture longer than the rest of them and still keep his mind busy.

Sister Mary Agnes hated an idle mind. She said it was the devil's workshop and a boy with an idle mind could commit the same kind of sin Adam committed in the Garden of Eden. Then, Sister Agnes said, what would the boy do most likely? — why he'd blame it on a girl, of course, just as Adam blamed original sin on Eve, and then finally the scribes would get hold of this, carry over the error from generation to generation. There was no stopping a lie once it was written, no stopping the evil that came from an idle mind.

But Stanley had never been punished for having an idle mind; he had learned how to squint, how to make colors and flashes of light fly through his brain. He could see millions of trees and branches, trillions of green leaves in the Garden of Eden. He could see creatures moving about with tails and snouts and floppy ears. He could see Adam, naked and strong; Eve, clad in a tiger skin, her long, lean legs. He could see the serpent, twisting and turning, braided with color. It was easy for Stanley to keep his mind busy because he knew he had an imagination. He was more proud of this than anything he could do, more proud than holding his pee until recess, his bowels until he walked all the way home after school.

Nearing the end of prayer, Stanley had an itch on the side of his nose. He could barely feel it, but it was there bothering him like a little insect scratching there, tickling him. Stanley kept his mind busy, brought in colors to go with the green of the trees, the braided hues of the snake. Purples and oranges, yellows for fruits on the trees, blues for clouds going by overhead, lavenders for light streaks, for the softness and pleasantness of Eden. But one of Stanley's hands disengaged from the other, came up to his nose and scratched. Scratched. Then it went right back, interlocked and folded on his desk without bothering him hardly at all.

Immediately, over on the girls' side of the room, Beatrice Skowronski's hand went up.

Sister Agnes, veiled in black, her head framed by her habit, sitting at her desk in the front of the room, looked over. "Yes, Beatrice, you may rise."

Beatrice stood, her knees pressed together, her mouth all grim-lipped. She spoke solemnly, "Proszem Wielebna Siostra (Blessed Sister, if I may), Stanley Merski is not praying. Stanley Merski has an idle mind."

"Are you sure, Beatrice?" Sister Agnes asked.

"Yes, Sister, I am sure."

Stanley could not believe this. Beatrice sometimes acted stupid, all the boys knew this, but she wouldn't lie. She knew well enough that of all the boys in class Stanley was the one who did not have an idle mind.

Sister Agnes opened her top desk drawer, pulled out her ruler. "Thank you, Beatrice, you may take your seat. Stanley, is it true that you are not praying, that you have an idle mind?"

Stanley's face got hot, prickled all over. He could not believe this at all. Sister Agnes was taking what Beatrice Skowronski said seriously. Sister was slapping her ruler into her palm. Slap, slap, slap. Stanley raised his hand, was given permission to rise.

"Proszem . . . Wielebna . . . Siostra."

"Yes, Stanley, speak."

"Sister, uh, I do not have an idle mind. Beatrice Skowronski is not telling the truth about me. No, Sister."

Sister Agnes slapped her ruler against her desk. SLAP! She turned to Beatrice. "Beatrice, do you wish to give an answer to this? Stand up."

Now Stanley felt better. Sister was yelling at Beatrice now. What answer could Beatrice give to this?

Beatrice rose, spoke in a level, controlled voice. "Sister, while Stanley Merski was supposed to be praying, I saw him scratch his nose. He did it, Sister. I saw him with my own two eyes."

"Stanley, did you scratch your nose?"

So this is all it was? Beatrice had seen something but had not understood. She was always making dumb mistakes like this.

Stanley spoke up; he would clarify. "Yes, Sister, I scratched my nose, but—"

"Beatrice, you may sit. Stanley, to my desk!" Again Sister Agnes slapped her ruler against her desk. SLAP!

At first Stanley did not move. He knew he could keep his mind full under any conditions. When he scratched, his mind was not idle. He wanted to tell Sister Agnes that he had taught himself to squint, to bring colors and visions and flashes of light into his mind. He could see the Garden of Eden, the things that were there . . .

"But, Sister—"

"Stanley, to my desk!" Sister Agnes repeated.

Stanley's knees bent, his body leaned forward. He moved to the desk.

"On the desk, Stanley." Sister Agnes pointed to his hand.

Stanley wanted to protest, there was a mistake here, but his lips stuck together. He could not speak.

Sister Agnes reached out, her hand cold and slippery like a snake, grabbed him by the wrist. With her other hand, she raised the ruler. It was long and thick, larger than Stanley's ruler. There was a thin metal edge that ran the length of it, pencil marks on the wood, nicks, gouges, little blotches of paint, red marks. Stanley had never seen these things from his desk. He watched the ruler. Sister Agnes slapped the flat part against the back of Stanley's hand. SLAP!

There was shock. "Sister!" Stanley said. Sister Agnes was hitting Stanley because she thought incorrectly that he had an idle mind. "Do not—" Sister's voice broke. "Do not let the devil speak through you, Stanley!"

Sister brought the ruler up higher than before, brought it down more sharply. SLAP!

This hurt. This hurt more than big John Jurczyk's whipping you with his fat fingers in paper, rock, and scissors. This, this . . . God!

The ruler went up again. Down. Up again. Down. Sister hit Stanley again and again.

Now,. there was pain, intense, sharp. It went through muscle and the thin little bones on the top of the hand. Stanley wanted to pull his hand away. There was jerking that began under his arm, ran to his hand.

But Sister Agnes must have felt this jerking, because she hit him again and again and again.

With the other boys this hitting was usually the end of punishment. Sister Agnes would breathe hard, her nose sucking air, her nostrils flaring; she would point and nod and turn. The boys would walk to their seats, eyes down, ears red, tears on their faces. But with Stanley Sister Agnes was not finished.

"Stanley, tell me, do you have an idle mind?"

Stanley wished he could say yes. Bernie Koczela could easily say yes. He didn't mind having an idle mind, lying, taking the name of the Lord in vain, coveting, lots of things. Bernie Koczela could later say, "Next time that fuck Sister hits me, I'm going to brain the son-of-a-bitch." Bernie Koczela could say yes, very easily, to stop her hitting. But Stanley could not. His hand was red and purple. The veins stuck up from his skin. There was a funny bump on his hand, round, like a little spotted egg.

"No, Sister," Stanley said.

"No, Stanley? Did you say no?"

Stanley shook his head, no.

Sister Agnes brushed past Stanley, went to the heat duct in the front of the room. She raised the metal grillework, swung it open. "Stanley!" she waved her ruler wildly, pointed inside.

Stanley moved forward, bent down, crawled inside. Sister replaced the grillework.

It was black in the duct, hot and dusty. There was the smell of coal, acrid, rank, sulphurous. Stanley's nose filled, twitched, dripped liquid. He backed himself up against the bulwark, pulled his knees up to his chest, sobbed.

"Stop that noise, Stanley!" Sister Agnes hollered.

Then Stanley heard Sister speaking to the class. "Without contrition," Sister was saying, "the devil's path is clear. Things are easy for him. At the first hint of sin, he hovers about. Then with sin, he is on us, grasping for us, trying to pull us under. Even the

Archangel Gabriel, even the Blessed Virgin Mary, the Son, the Father, the Holy Ghost, all the Saints, without contrition they have difficulty coming to our defense. The devil has the advantage in the battle of souls. In Stanley's case, the devil can come unimpeded and carve his mark on him, into his forehead or his chest, with a hot burning coal. Note well, Beatrice Skowronski, maintain your goodness. Note well, Bernie Koczela, Walter Wnuk, and Chester Olszowy, the devil is a violent, unrelenting foe . . ."

Stanley shut out Sister's voice, squinted his eyes, made himself see colors and flashes of light — lavender, jade green, ivory, violet, gold and silver. He imagined Adam and Eve, the serpent, glorious giant ferns, the trees, the fruit on the trees in the Garden of Eden. He raised his bruised and swollen hand to the soft skin of his face; it went right up without bothering him. He felt his throbbing hot veins, the little round egg raised on his skin. He imagined he was a scribe, writing with a long feathered quill. He began to make up his own stories about how the world began. There were lots of little children playing on green lawns, running after each other. There were animals and birds that spoke to the children. The sun and the stars shone at once together in the sky. Clouds were blue and red and pink. The children's cheeks were rosy. They laughed in musical notes. The animals protected them from the Devil, from the Holy Trinity, from all the Angels and Saints who made children feel guilty in play. Stanley's mind was busy, not idle. A white bird flew from behind a pink cloud; it landed on Stanley's hand, laid a small, sparkling egg. This was the egg of truth, and the animals came over to protect it, circling Stanley until he was safe and warm. Beatrice Skowronski was not there. Sister Agnes was not there. Stanley rubbed his face against the back of his hand, against his throbbing hot veins, against the little egg. He rubbed and he rubbed.

David Jauss

Apples

In memory of my grandmother, Agnes Konieczny

After Henry died, his wagon full
of unsold sewing machines and snow,
she moved to a house so small

she had to share the one bed
with my infant mother
and my aunt. My uncles slept

on the kitchen floor, warmed
by the woodstove, till May
when they lugged their blankets

out to the old Packard, up on blocks
in the backyard. Some mornings
they woke in the gray light and saw her

already hanging out other people's wash
for her fifty cents a basket. It took
half that first year just to pay

for his burial and eighteen more
to put the last of her children,
my mother, through school. But I knew

none of this, so I did not understand why,
picking apples for pies, she chose
only those that had fallen. Though I offered

to climb up and pick the reddest for her,
she knelt under the tree, her face
grim beneath her straw hat, and silently

filled her apron . . .
Only today, watching my wife
roll out piecrust, did I finally see

the apples on my grandmother's sill,
russet in the sun
slanting through the open window,

their bruises turning to cider.

Anna Wasescha

Babushka

All this land
flat like a good hard bed
and boundaried by stands of pine
and now
at the end of October
by fierce reds and golds
trees everywhere
You are Now Entering the Minnesota Forest Areas
on this road
going home to say goodbye
for the last time
to my grandmother
these crazy bright colors everywhere
like Lucille says an old woman
putting on makeup
how wide and flat this land is
how easy to imagine them
coming here in the first place
looking for other Polish-speaking people
settling twice before they found Perham
good soil, a church, a familiar tongue
how they came here
by horse and wagon
to lie down at night in their log house
a wall of pines to the North
to keep them warm
lakes on all sides
good land to raise wheat and potatoes
to raise children and grandchildren
today, as many as can
are coming home

I have in my heart pieces of
that peasant woman
her sheets crisp from ironing
her peonies, the Orange Crush in the old box
the two pails of fresh well water
next to the pantry sink

I have in my heart this land
flat and wide
in which I plan to lie when it is my time
all these little pieces of so
long ago wrap together
make a child's bed this is
a place where my childhood goes
on without me and
where death comes to put us down
to rest for long winters
for the long winter
which is soon to come and
which has lit these trees on fire

My mother says: the road to Perham gets shorter every year

Linda Mizejewski

Keeping My Name

Love shouldn't make it vanish,
yet the aunts and grocers,
even my father, banker of the syllables—
saw it float away like the Holy Ghost
at the moment of incarnation.

I've filled its crackly skeleton—
the long-boned initial,
the silent pelvic consonants—
for thirty years. Now I hold it
like stolen goods, and talk fast
with excuses.

How could I grow another one,
or bury this floppy chassis—
clanky, ornery, often fractured,
poked out on the classroom lists
like a sturdy, exotic weed?

Still, in someone's book
I am Mrs. Other.
The fine print spells it out—
never maiden, never
no one's girl. Like
my mother's mother,
reading and writing
no language, no name:
her X on her papers
marks the spot
where we disappear:
our names the crossbones
of the plucked-out ribs.

Keith Abbott

Raspberry Apparitions

Part Two

My mother met my father
up in the Wisconsin woods
& he went crazy for her
She didn't like him at first
He was hairy, she said
& "had long ropy arms,
like an ape,
from all that rowing
in the Navy racing crew."

She once said to me
matter-of-factly (but I heard
the awe & wonder & pride
still in her voice)
   "Well you know,
    Keith,
   your father
   was just *nuts*
    about me, he
   wouldn't leave
   me alone.

   I had *my*
     hands full
   getting *him* calmed down"

I guess she did *that*
    the way she wanted,
      too

    *   *   *

My Uncle John let the name slip
             "Now Firpo," he said,
—and then, seeing my puzzled face,
"You didn't *know* your dad
                 was called Firpo?
Oh yeah, they called Len Firpo
because all he liked to do was fight.
You heard of Louis
Firpo, the bull of the Pampas,
haven't you?
the Argentine heavyweight?
               (Men called Len
               Bull, too.)
Well, in Wisconsin during his logging days,
him and his pals they liked to
go to dances & start fights &
take away other men's girls.
       That's about when he met Gerts.
Once they got hitched,
she laid down the law: '*No more fights*'
       And he obeyed, only
       when he was first working on the docks
       there was this big Swede
       in Len's crew and
       that Swede knew Gerts
       had laid down the law,
       so he was taunting your dad.
       They were supposed to be working
       and the Swede told the crew
           '*Oh let Abbott do it,*
           he knows better than us.'
       That Swede was jealous
       because Lenny had been picked
       to be leadman out of that group.
       And your dad—even though he
       was foreman—
       he had to put up with that guff.

Well then, Gerts went back
        to St. Paul
and your dad sort of
        interpreted
                the rule
        to mean *no*
    fighting
if she was around.

Well, he was the foreman, so
on Friday after work,
he invited that Swede out on the dock,
drove him to his house,
carried him to his back door,
& threw him in to his missus.
Len told her, '*Make sure
he's to work on Monday.*'
                (She had *her* work cut out for her,
                let me tell you, getting
                her husband back on his feet)

Lenny never had
        any more trouble
                with his crews.

Gerts heard about it when
she returned but she figured
sometimes you weather a storm
by turning your back.

But Len loved her & he'd
given his word
so that was the last,
                that was the last."

On a visit I uncovered the photo
  album
        of their trip West
"Aunt Dot and Joe and Len and myself,
we had to come,
there was no work."
            in a model A words
                  & paint all over it

"Sick Cylinders" on the hood
"No springs, honest weight"
            "Mrs. Frequently" on the doors
                  "Badly bent but not broke"

Parked beside a stream in Montana
  a sapling bent
            over above the car
            the four banger
          engine hanging
"Your Uncle Joe
could fix any car
      made
        and catch trout in a stream
      that you could step across
but we only got
  as far as Washington, look at us,
all covered with paint & dust
            just like a bunch of hippies"

None of them
            married and the album
        a secret
                  until she didn't care
anymore

"Oh I can remember the roll down
the Cascade grade in neutral,
I was sitting on the fender
          with a flashlight —
                    our headlights out —
your dad & Joe cheering —
      all I could think about
              was that first hot bath"

                    ❊   ❊   ❊

She had dreamt of something else
"I was working as an accountant then
          & when I quit,
                    the woman I worked for
                              asked me to throw
                                        in as her partner
but your dad didn't want me
          to work
as long as he had a job
          & so I said no.
Having a job & supporting a
family was important
                    for Len, for all the men
then, it was still the Depression.
Still, I can't help   but wonder"

                    ❊   ❊   ❊

She told me with rue how
when Len brought her
                    to their new home
outside of Tacoma
                    a couple of acres
          & a half-finished shack
with ferns growing up through the floor

She sat down & cried

Of all her sisters she was the only
                          one to
end up on a farm

            A stump ranch a couple of cows
        a field full of raspberries
                        not much else

            *   *   *

On raising kids
during the Depression she said:
"*Why our friends thought we were
nuts*!
            *There wasn't enough
                        for any new mouths*!

*We had a hard drinking bunch
            & once we had the first two
they stopped coming
            around*

We had to get new friends

            *But that wasn't hard—
everyone loved Len
            at social do's*"

            *   *   *

"Everyone loved
Len
at social do's"
The most erotic
I've ever seen
My father was when
he was talking
(as a man might—
with that familiar
Irish geniality)
Enjoying a woman's
wit
& warmth

"Len always brought out
the best in people"
mom said
(My perception of
eroticism too)
"We had more invitations
than we had time.
It got so
we had to turn
people down.
Life with your dad
was always so full."

*   *   *

She lived alone
in a suburban home
she & my father bought before
his death

Once I visited her
        & I was tired after dinner
so I went into the living room
          to lie down

She must have thought
        I went down the hall
to the bedroom she came in it was dusk & drew
          the red curtains quite
              oblivious
to me

I watched her move
          around the grey
      living room
          an apparition
stained red by the light through
          the drapes
& I thought
      this is what it
          must be like
      for her, now

Olivia Diamond

The Butter Churn

We were city people. After World War II, when my grand-mother was able to visit Poland, she brought back a wooden knick-knack, probably carved by some mountaineer in the Polish Carpathians. It was probably 1950. I was three when I first laid eyes on this souvenir of her journey by oceanliner back across the Atlantic. My mother related when I was much older how grandmother, Babcha we called her, had so looked forward to the journey. I carried my grandmother's passport photo in my wallet until a few years ago when my purse was stolen. The snatcher took no money, but for days I felt robbed of my heritage. Now, I have an enlargement of that photo before me. She did not par-ticularly look happy in that photo, but in passport pictures, no matter what the anticipation, the expressions are grim. My mother told me that on her return grandmother said, "I'm glad to be back. I'll never go there again."

It was a confirmation that she had been in America too long, ar-riving at age 16 in 1906. She married shortly thereafter, tried farming for a year with my grandfather, the son of a Polish land-owner, in Ladysmith, Wisconsin. The venture lasted just long enough for my uncle to be born on that farm. Complaining of the bitter winter, she returned to Chicago, where my grandfather tried his luck at a corner grocery. I can still see the photo of the pair taken in that ill-lighted store. Grandfather in white apron, stood behind a pastry counter, a tall, dark-haired man. What a woman would term "a fine figure of a man," and my shorter, rounder grandmother stood by the cash register. Like the farming venture, this business was short-lived, and grandfather wandered into various jobs in factories while Babcha, a fine seamstress, went to work in the clothing factories.

So why did Babcha bring back the butter churn? I spent hours in a maroon stuffed chair working its dasher up and down, wondering how butter really was made. How did all this churning produce butter? I wondered the more as Babcha sat me down to lunch, spread pale yellow Land 'O Lakes butter from a tub across two thick slabs of dark rye bread. I studied the placid cows on the butter tub, the butter churn still a mystery to me. Babcha was a city girl from Danzig. Why a butter churn?

When I was six and finally had spending money in my dress pocket — it was all of a dollar — I was elated I could buy a Mother's Day present. It was the first one I remember getting. We lived in a tenement on Hermitage Avenue in Chicago. Grandmother had retired and sold her house. I went to the corner gift shop. My first thought was to get some kind of knick-knack. It had to be for a dollar.

The first object that caught my eye was a creamer cow with wonderful udders. It was dappled brown and white and I knew I had to have it. "That one," I said. "How much?"

"89 cents."

Thirty-two years later, at the Ramada Inn in Rockford, Illinois, I sat down before a psychic artist who was doodling on a drawing pad. For $15.00, he would give me a visual reading, sketching on his pad with a brown crayon as he caught my vibrations. He didn't say much, promised me no money, no new job or lover. After five minutes, he turned his pad to me. I saw a butter churn.

"Why a butter churn?" I stammered.

"You're a butter churn," he replied. "Your mind is constantly churning."

He turned the pad toward him and continued drawing. A few seconds later, he turned the pad toward me again and asked, "Do you know this woman?"

I recognized the face immediately.

"Yes, it's my grandmother." It was the sober countenance in her passport picture.

"Well, she's your spirit-guide."

I went home with the rolled-up drawing in my hand. I searched for a large glass frame for the drawing — a brown crayoned sketch of a woman with a butter churn in the upper right background. I hung it in my dining room and studied the small eyes and dignified chin of this woman who also had written poetry and her brother's memoirs. He was a soldier heavily decorated by the Polish government, who had escaped from imprisonment in Siberia to find refuge in America. Did she know that the little girl sitting in her parlor working the dasher up and down was dreaming of long-haired maidens letting down their hair, of muscular aerialists in white tights catching their pretty partners before they fell, and of genies with bulging eyes promising to fly her to Baghdad? Did she surmise the girl who never spoke unless spoken to dreamed of dressing her world in words?

I've traveled, it's true, to far-away places—to Cordoba, Cairo and Marrakesh. But I've come home to the Midwest I love to write those novels and poems which have been churning within me, where I sit and talk in my mother's kitchen and where my eye catches the cow creamer she has preserved over the years on top of her refrigerator.

"Mom, where is that wooden butter churn Babcha brought back from Poland?"

She looked at me, interested. "I still have it. Why?" she answered.

"I really liked it," I answered, hoping I did not sound like I was coveting it.

"I'll get it." She reached in a cupboard, brought out the butter churn and handed it to me. "If you like it so well, it's yours when I'm gone. Babcha wrote like you. I'll never forget the beautiful poem she wrote in Polish about her dead child."

Wordlessly, I worked the dasher up and down.

Arlene Maass

Primary Grades

born on the brink of the Korean war
a thank-you dr. saulk pinch in the arm
traipsing to Fern Hill for kindergarten
chewing pink Brooklyn gum
Israelis and Egyptians fight in the Sinai
and i don't know war
i do know wet-bed trauma and being ugly as argyle
and fear is a marble nun with steel pinz nez
chalking black slate with atomic dust
ranks of nuns—a phalanx—
armed with dogma and yardsticks
discussing the dispensation of grace
riveting the young and the dense
with black rosary bead eyes
throwing me into fascination
printing letters like black boughs against white light
who colors cherry blossoms in Hiroshima
yellow and black triangles mark
the air raid shelters
when the hard rain falls
we will be in the basement of Sacred Heart of Jesus

learning to read
mispronouncing words as if chewing on a panatela
a lisp was snared and gawked at after school
with a semi-skilled therapist
teaching little runts to write
their Polish surnames in rotunda letters
pushing a lead pencil to the blue lines
Hungary is invaded by the Russians
ferrying on to another practice page,
clodhopping through primers
behemoth kid with chapped lips
brain-dead in math
dreaming with lard eye whites

laughing silently like a good catholic
larry curlie & moses hiding behind the catechism
who was that german with the black comb moustache?
moonstruck by the chow-chow of words, words—
learning to read
means the round new world has been found.

Mary was bovine but smart to the point of puke
beef boullion cube eyes saying see? see?
it was her pocket-size sister
a li'l bijou with brick brown eyes
that i called my best friend, the Polish pygmie
slaughtering Chopin on the upright
while the world practiced madness into November
for all saints day and all souls day
so gray gold and black the clouds around pyramids
why did god let jews die in ovens?
howling at the autumn leaves,
maybe that's when i heard a still small voice
and turned to chase after books.

Eichmann sits in a dock of glass
and will hang from a mustard tree
over there in Jerusalem
does the devil wear horned rimmed glasses
is satan a german engineer, Gesu, Maria, Yosef?
who can answer my question?
math was more awful than religion
and what is the sense of
taking words and sentences apart
splitting more atoms
why is learning like squirting citrus on a canker sore?
i took out the window to Kinnikinnic Avenue
and think about people who jumped from windows
over a wall in Berlin
wondering whatever happened to the Indians
at all our bending kneeling dirty rivers

all we let them leave us were funnier words
than keilbasa and babushka and dupa
words like milwaukee pewaukee and ouzakee
words that'll make you more dizzy
than 10 boilermakers at AmVet's Hall
and who is Fidel Castro with the burnt toast beard?
Friday afternoon smelled like Elmer's glue
and a powder burn

a short November day trapped in a flue
trapped in a whining corridor
Sister Naomi got on the blower to proclaim
with great sadness his death
and the smirkers counted the asses
in assassination

another chance to pray for the dead;
another chance to crawl into the basement
of the Sacred Heart of Jesus.

K. C. Frederick

What Can You Do with a Fish?

O h, sweet Christ, Art sang to himself, relaxing at last, lying against the cool bark of a willow. He could hardly believe it was there on the grass; but for a while he kept from looking because he wanted to hold it in his mind. Sweet Christ, he repeated, feeling his cut hand already beginning to heal, his soggy trousers drying in the warm air, his rundown nerves and muscles recharging in the rich blank moment of complete exhaustion. Finally he looked and saw it, large and strange like a hunk of meteorite, but even seeing it didn't convince him it was really his: it couldn't be his because the old Polacks who came out there every weekend never caught anything that big, and he was no fisherman. And to have got it with that old rod and reel, weak line, no net, so that he had to get into the water after it and cut his hand on its gill—no, it couldn't be his, but there it was, lying there as long as a man's leg, powerful, vicious-looking, a strange thing to find in the grass with its hard, pirate's eye that was designed to search out swimming perch and frogs, its strong tail and fins slapping pointlessly now at the thin air.

It belonged in the cold water far below the river's green skin, not in the soft, bright late afternoon heat. When he first glimpsed it it had looked like a fully preserved dinosaur under the ice— now he closed his eyes and saw it glowing in the high grass like an oddly shaped moon, and the moment hung: he could feel the tree shift its weight in the breeze. He pressed the cool grass to his cut hand and tried to recapture appropriate phrases from those hundreds of stories he'd read when he was thirteen, in magazines like *Field and Stream* and *Sports Afield*, but the words just reminded him of the barbershops he'd read them in. He opened his eyes and saw the water again. He reached cautiously toward his shirt pocket. There was one twisted cigarette left— he would have been willing to trade the contents of his wallet for that one smoke—and he lit it hungrily. Now, sucking down the dry, friendly smoke, he had everything: if the bomb came he wouldn't flinch. But it would be even better if the bomb held off for a while yet. He watched a dragonfly silently grasp a blade of grass. It stuck there, wings extended stiffly like transparent jacknife blades. Somewhere in the distance a motorboat was droning in a hidden bay. A breath of wind cooled his face. He inhaled again and looked at the fish.

But he started to remember troubles again and all the empty crates that filled his mind: he and Rita were through for good and nothing had taken its place; high school was over and he had nothing to do; he was going to the Navy for no good reason; and he'd come out here only because he was bored, and it would be a way of killing time. He bent forward and looked steadily at the pike—it was at least a yard long; the white, rectangular spots gleamed like coins on its green sides. He was tired, but he suddenly felt he should be doing something, so he picked himself up. When the fish smacked at the grass with its tail, he used the rake to pull it into the shade. Then he ripped out some of the longer tufts, soaked them, the closed cut pinching a little, and threw them over the fish. The shade and moisture would keep it alive longer. He stood there a few moments looking at the long white dock extending into the deep, swift part of the river where he'd first hooked it. He tried to judge how long it had actually taken to land the fish: the incredible, nerve-wringing experience had seemed to take forever, but once it was over, he could only think of it as quick and surprising, it had caught him before he was ready for it. He realized it couldn't have taken more than ten minutes. It was hard to believe, and he realized that already he was losing the experience, that all he had left was a story in his own mind that was becoming blurred. All he had was his own word for it. But of course, he had the fish.

The pike flapped again, the grass sticking to its sides. Art saw that it was dying. All at once he felt a need to get back to Detroit while it was still alive, as if the fish were a wounded gangster who had to be taken to the cops so he could talk before he died. He tossed away his cigarette and ripped out more grass, soaked it, strewed it all around the pike: it looked like a fancy meal. Satisfied he had enough covering, he filled his cupped hands with water and poured it over the grass. He got some newspaper and wrapped the fish in it so that the moisture would be held in. He wished he'd had a tarpaulin, that would have been even better. When he picked up the wrapped fish, he felt its full weight for the first time. It was heavy; once again he wondered that he'd been able to land it. He put it in the car's trunk, where at least it would be protected from the sun.

He was ready to go now, and he should have got into the car, but he felt a hesitation. Everything was so perfect that any change could only be for the worse. He leaned against his uncle's old car, and the warm metal felt good. He felt lucky, rewarded. Every break had gone right in his fight with the fish, and even the things that had made it hard just added to the victory. Everything he'd done had been smart. The shaggy willows swayed in the warm breeze, and he wished he could stop time for five minutes or so while he added things up. This was the kind of experience that might start a lucky streak. He must have done something in the last hour that was the key to everything, if he could only remember it. Something inside his head had clicked—a broken windshield wiper had got working for a moment. He was used to having the glass blurred, and he couldn't be sure the wipers would keep working. He touched the warm door of the car's trunk: he had a trophy. He felt like an especially smart crook.

But once he was under way, his mood began to sink. As he drove over the quiet, dusty road to the ferry, as the orange ferry pulled him across the swift, deep river (he could never forget when he crossed that there was supposed to be a boatload of bootleg whiskey down there, ninety feet below), as he started along the curve of the lake toward the city, his mind kept nibbling away at the question; what do you do with something like this, a trophy, a prize? There was a bar in Detroit that served things like buffalo burgers and rattlesnake steaks. He'd seen a menu once, and what he remembered best was that for a whole group that rented the place for a banquet of, say, lion meat, they'd show films of the hunt. Art had forgotten whether the films came before or after the meal, and he wasn't sure which would have made him sicker. But for a moment he imagined himself presiding over a big fish dinner (except that he didn't eat fish) and then, when they'd cleared away the plates, they'd roll down the screen and show him catching his monster pike, jumping in after it, cutting his hand on the inside of the fish's gill (it had been a small cut, but as he imagined it in the film, it was like an oil leak), and finally pulling the pike out of the water with the rake.

But it was too much—he had to work too hard at it—it was like the football banquets he used to imagine before he started high school: the All-State awards he got there never really consoled him for barely being a regular on the actual team. It seemed, now that high school was over, just as incredible that these long, boring years were past, as that the catching of the fish had actually taken just a few minutes: before high school he'd dreamed of being a football star, of doing vaguely exciting things with the same kids he'd known all his life, but when it happened, it was all wrong. Even if he had been a football star, no one would have cared very much—it was the tough guys who were the heroes, the guys who started fights after the games, and would become numbers men when they left school—and Art wasn't tough. In fact, he knew that by his senior year he was considered pretty dull—you were either one or the other—and though he tried to hide it, and never got very good grades, the other kids knew he actually liked to read, and to learn. And so, with high school over, all his imaginary football banquets were ended, and he was just another Polack in Detroit.

The trouble with everything was, no matter how good it might make you feel, sooner or later you had to come back to Detroit, and that spoiled it. Detroit was the taste in his mouth as he chewed on a greasy hamburger in the drive-in, slowly, without appetite, because he found now that he was in no hurry to get anywhere, he was no longer bringing his fish in against a deadline. He watched a short blonde carhop dancing by herself in the corner to the blaring juke-box music and somehow it seemed sad. He was still feeling this way by the time he got to the city. As he moved along one of the big streets, the traffic was mostly gone, and only a few cars raced noisily past him on the broad asphalt plain between dull, slouching buildings. High windows were stuffed full of liquor, lawnmowers, baseball bats, and cars that looked shiny and dead. Everywhere were giant letters and numbers, big enough to be read even as you zipped by. There were words like Avco, Goldman, Nova, Northeast — pasted on windows — objects in themselves, blotting out the merchandise as though the words themselves were for sale. Art knew that if he were to stop the car in the middle of the street right now and lay the fish down there, on the pavement, no one would even notice this not very large cylinder with a head and tail. The cars would pass it, run right over it (he could hear the thunks), flattening it, dulling it, until it was just a thin layer on the pavement, to be washed away in the next good rainstorm and less durable than Avco or Nova.

Turning off the wide street, he was in the city of houses. Every-thing was quiet, just after dinner, and people were sitting around their tables, digesting their food. It was still bright but there was no energy behind the light now. House after wooden house was crossed by the shadow of the house next door, the shapes moving past thickly, opening out at corners and intersections where a few kids sat blankly on the steps of neighborhood groceries or bakeries. Then the house-shapes again, hung with wedges of shadow. Lines of tired cars sprawled before porches. Steel, wood, glass, brick, rubber. There were smells in the street too: asphalt, the dead rotting heat — even the trees and grass gave off the smell of intersection. He was tired, and he tried to remember if there was a Tiger game on TV tonight that he could use to wipe out the night.

By the time he was back in the neighborhood his lonely excite-ment over the fish embarrassed him. He felt he'd been driving a hearse all day and all he wanted to do was get rid of the body. Half-heartedly he tried Eddie Galicki's place, but as he guessed, Eddie was out with Virge somewhere. So much for showing off his catch. Even so he was a little relieved. It seemed pretty stupid now to be driving around with a fish, trying to show it to someone. What could you expect them to say? All that was left was to go to his Uncle Gabby's to return the car. It was as good a place as any to get rid of the pike. Not that his uncle needed it or could use it. Art had already had to give him two dollars for the use of his car, and that was enough for him to get drunk on, which was his only real need. Except for the odd electrical jobs he did, he hadn't worked in years; yet somehow he always managed to pick up enough change to be able to buy a few drinks at Connie's bar, get a few bought for him, and sit around complaining. He insulted all the customers but nobody took him seriously enough to fight him; though if they had, he probably wouldn't have been hurt, scrawny as he was. He stepped into a passing car once and he wasn't even scratched; and another time he completely wrecked his brother's car but walked away clean. Everybody called him a loser but he was a funny kind of loser. In his own way, he had it made, except for his wife, who was as big as a barn and really mean when she got drunk, and once pushed him down his front steps. He survived that too, but sometimes when he limped you could tell he was thinking about it.

In front of his uncle's house, he opened the trunk and saw that the fish was still alive though all it could manage now was a slow, mechanical opening and closing of its gills. The water still glistened. As he lifted his prize, Art marveled again at how heavy it was; it was amazing that something that big shouldn't be worth more. His uncle ought to at least give him back a dollar for the fish, or maybe let him use the car free tomorrow. But Art knew better: with the few people he had any power over, his uncle wasn't soft.

Art was on the porch Uncle Gabby had been pushed from. (It had only happened once, but in his mind he saw the old man getting thrown down again and again, slow motion, his mouth a dark cave with curses escaping like flying bats.) Holding the soggy bundle across his arms, his pants still damp below the knees, Art knocked on the door but no one answered, and he had to keep knocking, which was hard to do with the fish in his arms. He was getting angry now. He knew his uncle was home. All he wanted to do was to get rid of the damned fish — the thought of dumping it in the garbage can in the alley crossed his mind — he'd leave his uncle's keys on the porch and go home, take a shower and change, But he knew he couldn't do it, so he suffered and rapped, still louder, until at last he heard the sudden snapping open of the door and saw his uncle, hunched over, squinting, trying to squirm free of sleep, and holding the door knob for support. "Aw, for Christ's sake, it's you," he croaked, shaking the fuzz out of his head. His body seemed to be falling slowly in several directions at once, but his bloodshot eyes made a quick, suspicious leap past Art toward the car. "Goddam car's covered with dust," he mumbled. "What'd you do? Race it over that dirt road?" He always assumed that everyone was trying to screw him. Even while he talked, though, his eyes crawled back into their red webs and he seemed to have forgotten where he was. His sing-song voice trailed off into a distant humming, and Art continued to stand there, with the wet, heavy fish in his arms. The man hadn't even noticed it: Art felt like taking it by the tail and bringing it down on his uncle's head; but the old man finally staggered back into the dark house, leaving the door open behind him, and Art could do nothing but follow.

Inside, the house smelled thickly of his uncle's failure. Art moved through the dark living room full of holy pictures Aunt Sophie collected, and sometimes threw at her husband. Even when she wasn't home, she left her presence all over the place, like the tracks of some large animal. In the kitchen, Uncle Gabby had dropped himself before a tableful of dirty dishes. The place was a mess as usual. The evening light illuminated a little star of cellophane under the table and a powder of crumbs shining on a chair. "Oh, Christ," his uncle slurred, and took a sip of cold coffee. "What the hell have you got there?" he suddenly asked, noticing the wet hulk that Art carried awkwardly before him.

"It's a fish," Art said, not too hopefully.

"A fish?" The older man frowned. "What the hell you bring it in here for?"

Though it was clumsy with one hand, Art managed to pull away the mushy paper and brush back the grass, revealing the huge, vicious head of the pike, near dead, the long slits of mouth open enough to show the dangerously plentiful teeth. "Look," he said, pushing it toward his uncle like a proud mother showing a baby. Just a glimpse of the head was enough to recall the fear he'd felt just before dropping off the dock into the water. "You want it?" he asked, trying to act casual.

"What the hell do I want with a Goddamned fish?" he shouted. "Get that thing out of here." He waved it away, hardly looking at it, and took up his coffee cup. "Put it down somewhere," he growled. "Don't just stand there like an idiot. Put it in the sink."

Art carried his load to the sink full of dirty dishes and set it down noisily atop the half-full cups and watermelon rind. It was so long its uncovered tail hung out over one edge; he'd had to move the dish-drying tray and set its head on the dirty rubber mat with little channels that caught its runoff. "It's too big," he said, knowing his uncle wasn't listening, and he half-hoped that with one final surge of life the pike would knock the cups flying and fling the tray to the floor. But it just lay there while his uncle moaned curses into his coffee cup. From the alley behind the house came shouts of black kids playing.

"Here's the keys," Art muttered, dropping them to the table. But his uncle, lost in his own world, didn't hear him. He raised his head and looked out toward the front door. Just across the street the yellow bricks of the rectory shone through the screen. "God damned monsignor," he spat, hitting the table with his palm. He ran his hand through his hair. "Listen, kid, don't let those priests make a monkey out of you." Art was still wondering what brought that up when the old man switched directions, as if he'd just remembered something: "When the Hell you going to the Navy, anyway?"

He wished he knew. "They said I could go on active duty in a couple of months." He looked at the sink: the fish had already become part of the mess.

"You'll see," his uncle said, his voice reaching for the moralistic pitch. "All this free and easy stuff's going to be over. You're going to have to get up early in the morning. . ." But he suddenly lost interest and let it drop. Art was already far away. The sudden mention of the Navy reminded him that someday he'd be out of here.

He was trying to hold on to this feeling when suddenly his uncle wheeled back to another topic: "Mother fucking priests." His voice blazed. "God damned monsignor don't care if you don't go to church. But he sure knows if you're not putting something in the collection basket." Silently he meditated on some grievance with the monsignor: probably the pastor had been trying to influence some of the women of the parish not to do business with his uncle. "The bastard," he exclaimed.

"Oh, screw the monsignor," Art said quietly, not because he sided with his uncle, but because he was bored with his uncle's problems; he was like a bug, and almost anyone could step on him from his wife to the monsignor, and for his uncle to talk to him about it made it somehow Art's problem too.

"What should I do with the fish?" he asked.

"Get it out of here." His uncle's face sagged like a wet dishrag. "I don't want any God damned fish. Give it to one of those sports in the bar—" Suddenly his voice straightened as if it had been pinched. Without any transition he was saying excitedly, "Wait a minute . . ."

The last thing Art wanted to do was wait a minute. But his uncle got up now, laughing to himself, and looked at the oversized fish squeezed in among the dishes. "Hot damn," he said, slapping his hands, and he turned to Art with a sudden look of approval on his face. "Say, that *is* a mighty big fish, isn't it?" He walked to the sink and touched its tail. He stood before the pike, his head tilted as if it had come unscrewed. Art realized he should have guessed from the beginning what would happen: his uncle wanted to take the fish to Connie's bar and show it to the numbers men who'd be there—it might be worth a few free drinks. Art was tired; he saw now that from the moment he'd hooked it the fish had been getting its silent revenge. It had caused him nothing but trouble. Now he was to be turned over to this old man, to act as his altar boy, carrying the fish before him in their little procession. "No," he would have liked to say, "damn it, no. It's your fucking fish now; carry it yourself." But somehow he didn't. "I don't know," he said. The old man wasn't paying attention. As Art watched his uncle's calculating face, his curiosity was roused. He knew he'd deliver this package to the bar. But then what would his uncle do with the fish? Art saw it lying on the floor of the bar, dead, beginning to smell, and Uncle Gabby stopping every newcomer with the same story, hoping to get one last free drink before the bones began to show. In a way it would be interesting to see what happened: if the guys from the bar clouted him, that would be worth seeing too. But as he wet the grass and wrapped the fish in fresh newspaper, he realized that he too had been thinking of those numbers men in the bar, the high school tough guys of a few years ago. Maybe he'd wanted all along to show the fish to them. Was it possible that even as he lay back against the tree with the fish on the grass he was secretly hoping to use Uncle Gabby to get it into the bar, so that they could see it? Because he knew he was as much of a blank to the numbers men as his uncle: when he'd won a citywide essay contest in his junior year, they'd acted as if he'd been caught in some perversion.

It burned him to think, as he picked up the fish again, that his uncle was more real to them than he was. But one thing he was sure of: they couldn't ignore an actual fish this big.

When the two of them entered the bar, his blood thickened. The juke-box that washed over the buzz of voices, the smell of liquor and smoke, faint traces of perfume, the points of light and color softened by the haze, gave the place a kind of underwater feeling, and Art found himself, even with the heavy fish in his arms, adjusting to the rhythm of the place by relaxing his stance. He hesitated just inside the threshold for a moment, but his uncle pushed at him from behind. "Here, here," he rasped, and springing ahead, he pointed to a table. "Put it down there." But he seemed to forget about Art immediately, and stood there vacantly, waiting for someone to turn around. Art continued to hold the wrapped fish. Near them were four numbers men playing cards almost wordlessly. They were all big, and the tiny table squeezed between them like someone they'd jumped and knocked down, made them look even bigger. For a few seconds after Art's arrival, they remained locked in their game. Except for the flicker of their eyes when the door had been opened, they all stared down at the little table, intent, only breaking their silence with a grunt or half-audible curses, their broad backsides uneasy in the chairs while their big hands hid the little cards. Even Art's uncle seemed to have forgotten his plans for the moment, and stared over the thick backs of the players at their cards. Art remembered those backs, and the white hats that rose above them like shark fins, in the crowds after basketball games a few years ago. He suddenly felt embarrassed, standing before the table with his dripping package wrapped in newspaper. The bartender had noticed him and had started down the bar to find out what Art, a minor, was doing here. "I'm a paper boy," he felt like saying. "I've got some good news." Just then the hand ended with one of the men slamming his cards to the table, which set off a crack of laughter and swearing, and as the men pushed their chairs away from the table, Uncle Gabby stepped forward. "Hey, look at this," he called.

The card players turned sceptically toward the intruders, as though they feared Art was going to deliver a speech. They looked as if they expected to be bored, sitting there heavily, even their big relaxed fists sneering at him and his essay contests. He felt inadequately armed, even guilty. One of the men moved in his chair impatiently, as if he was about to say, "Hey. What the shit: let's get on with this game." So Art stepped forward and, not knowing what to say, he held the covered fish before him. The water had turned the print into an indecipherable blur.

"Here, you dumb ass-hole," his uncle barked. Art clenched his fist but his uncle didn't even know he was there. He grabbed at the paper and began tearing at it. "Look," he cried, ripping off the covering so that the fish's scales began to show. To Art, they seemed disappointingly dull. "There," his uncle said when he'd got the head free. The pike was dead now. "There. Look."

"Motherfuck," one of the cardplayers grunted, pushing back his chair so he could get up. The others did the same.

"Christ, where'd that come from?" another asked. They were really impressed. Taken by surprise, they forgot all about their cards and bottles.

"The kid got it at Big Johnny's," his uncle answered for him. Art was grateful at least that he didn't claim it for himself.

"At Big Johnny's? Where?" A large man bent over the fish but kept a careful space between himself and the pike's mouth.

"I was casting off the dock." It seemed like years ago.

By now they were all gathered around him and his uncle motioned for him to put the fish on the table, which he was glad to do. He'd had enough weight-lifting for one day.

"What is it? A muskie?" someone asked. A skinny old man at

the pool table wanted to keep playing, but his partner came over to join the crowd, and he just stood beside the pool table leaning on his stick.

"That's a pike, isn't it, Artie?"

Men came up from the bar to look at the fish and they all paid their tribute with hushed, reverent swearing. For the time being everyone seemed to have forgotten the presence of everyone else in the bar, including Art. They were all fascinated by the dead creature stretched across the table. It was like the time when there'd been a long streetcar strike and he and his friends had been standing on the corner talking: because he was facing the right way he was the only one to see an orange length slide into an intersection blocks away. When he pointed they all turned around and shouted the word for him: "A streetcar. A streetcar. For Christ's sake, it's a streetcar."

For a while, the customers were so interested in the fish that Uncle Gabby began to look around nervously, afraid they'd lost their taste for liquor. But at last someone ordered a round of drinks, and his face was wrung dry of worry. "Want a Coke?" he offered bigheartedly, but one of the numbers men cut him off: "Shit, man, he caught that fish; he can have a real drink." The bartender wasn't comfortable about serving minors but at last he let Art down a quick shot in the back room. When he came back the numbers men were excitedly talking about going to Big Johnny's tomorrow. "You know," one of them said, "the mate to that thing'll be right there, in the same spot." Anything that had to do with the outdoors would set off a bunch of Polacks. The old ones were always fooling with gardens and getting up at the crack of dawn to hunt mushrooms; and even when they went to Big Johnny's and sat on the dock all day listening to the ballgame and drinking beer, so that it was just like being in a bar, they felt better because it was outdoors. So it was no surprise that the younger numbers men would feel challenged by anything that had to do with hunting or fishing and would come out with statements like the one about the pike's mate, that even Art knew was nonsense. The fish lay on the table like a stick of firewood and for a few moments the bar was transformed into a hunting and fishing lodge and all of Detroit outside the bar's walls was a Northern wilderness. Even the reluctant pool player had been drawn into the fish stories and only Uncle Gabby was silent, though contented: his uncle was really an indoor person. He could have been born in a bar.

The dead fish looked smaller and duller, as if its effect on the group had cost it its remaining luster. It seemed all but forgotten as the numbers men competed with tales of their fishing prowess or their strategies for getting the mate they'd convinced themselves was lurking just off Big Johnny's dock. Occasionally someone would ask Art about details of his catch, and he gave back remembered phrases from outdoor magazines. They bought another round of drinks and Art went to the back room once more. He felt light now, not good, not elated. But not bad. He saw the numbers men talking with quick gestures; he saw his uncle drinking alone and thinking hard about something; he saw the fish lying on the newspaper, stone dead, its eye vacant: a fly was walking across its sticky side.

Suddenly his uncle rapped the table, poured down his drink and called to him. "Come on," he said, "I just had an idea." Art lifted himself, the whole day's weariness coming back to him. When he picked up the fish nobody noticed. The juke-box was blasting away and all over the bar people were busy talking to each other. Some of the customers turned their heads for a moment when Art covered the fish again, but the break in the bar's rhythm was slight, just as it had been when they'd entered; and he and his uncle slipped out quietly. When they were out in the dark street, the sounds from the bar, though quieter, seemed gayer, more emphatic on the warm night air. From the moment he'd got up, Art's spirits had been sinking: the liquor had given him an expansive feeling, but now he was aware of how empty those expanses were: it was like being in a giant phone booth. He regretted the drinks too, since there was no point to getting high if you couldn't do anything with it. From habit his mind turned toward Rita, but he knew that was a closed book. All he could do was to grit his teeth and stick it out to the end with this fish—it couldn't be long now. He was puzzled, though: why had his uncle left the bar, when there was probably at least one more free drink in it for him? The move had been so unpredictable that Art didn't even have any guesses handy, and would have to find out from the old man himself. He didn't have long to wait. "Listen," his uncle said, "I want you to take that fish to the monsignor."

Though they were near the bar, and some of the light reached out into the street, it was dark, and since his uncle had dropped his head when he stepped back, Art couldn't see his expression. Still, he could imagine the smile of triumph. His own face tightened in a reflection of that smile. The bastard! What a move! It was brilliant. It would get the monsignor off his back beautifully. Art thought of the biblical passage that had troubled him as a kid, about loving your enemies and heaping burning coals on them. Now he realized what he'd been carrying in his uncle's procession all this while: a couple of armsful of burning coals.

Art stood in the hall of the rectory, waiting for the monsignor. The warm, enclosed air had its own particular smell. Art had known it all his life: faintly sweet from incense, it was smooth, cleaned, empty of food, an impressive official aroma, unlike any other. It seemed to come from the paintings in the hall of Christ and the saints, pale, sad but quietly commanding men, thoughtful in their dim garments that blended into fading landscapes. It was the smell of power, of an efficient, womanless world of crosses, triangles, circles—clean symbols of an order visible everywhere in the ranks of priests, even in the makes of the cars they drove. There was a time when Art had wanted to be a priest: he'd been attracted to the Jesuits with their military rigor, with their generals and provincials; now he was going to the Navy only because Detroit was on no ocean. It had been four years ago that he'd come close to entering the seminary's high school, and his last-minute switch had been a disappointment to the monsignor: a priest from the parish would have been a feather in his cap. It was strange to think of himself as a priest, but even stranger to realize as he waited for him that the monsignor had his losses too, and that Art was surely one of them. Maybe the pastor would think Art owed him the fish for his desertion. It didn't matter. The important thing was that someone was getting the thing at last and the involvements it had gotten him into would be over. The need to get out of Detroit suddenly attacked him like heartburn. In the bar he'd thought he was a big deal for about thirteen seconds, but even as he'd downed the second drink in the back room he'd known that things don't change just because you catch a fish. It embarrassed him to think that he had. Now he wondered, did things ever change?

The monsignor came down the steps gravely, followed by Father Boris, who'd answered the door. He was a little grey priest from Poland, and he followed his boss at a respectful distance. Seeing him again, Art uttered a little prayer of thanks that he'd escaped that fate. It made him realize not everything was lost.

"Well, well, good evening, Arthur," the monsignor said impressively. The tall, smooth-looking priest wore his black cassock with a purple sash, but he had no power over Art.

"Hello, monsignor," he said quickly. "I've got this pike. My uncle Mr. Sendlik asked me to take it to you, monsignor." It was probably the liquor, but Art felt like saying "monsignor" again and again. When he'd mentioned his uncle's name, the priest's face, which was the color of strawberry ice-cream, lost its official smile of greeting, and just hovered there without any expression at all for a moment. He seemed to be weighing the possibilities of halting the affair now, before Art could unveil the fish, so he could keep his hold on Uncle Gabby; but the priest was a fisherman too, and his eyes betrayed his curiosity about what was obviously a giant fish under the paper. All at once something in the monsignor's face gave Art the idea that the pastor was getting some heat from the bishop, and was already thinking of using the pike in his own way. At last, bringing his hands together, the priest exclaimed, "Well, let's see it."

Once again Art displayed his fish. He was getting to be like a magician with his act, and this time he did it more slowly, deliberately. When he saw that dead familiar face again, Art was supremely bored: it was getting to be like the face of a relative. The pike seemed to him one of the dullest of God's creatures; but its power still worked on the priests. The monsignor's eyes enlarged quietly and Father Boris darted toward the revealed fish as if he was going to race his superior to a relic they both wanted to kiss; but, catching himself in time, he was content to stand on tip-toe just beside and slightly behind the monsignor.

The taller priest bent over the fish. "Oh, my. I'll say *that's* a big one." He rubbed his pink hands thoughtfully. "Mmm," he hummed softly, "I've been fishing thirty years and I've never got one that big."

"Just luck, monsignor," Art consoled him.

"Mmm . . .Your uncle sent . . ." He was looking at the dead fish, as if measuring it for his freezer, where he could keep it until he needed to spring it on the bishop.

"Yes, monsignor," Art doled out his words solemnly. "Mr. Sendlik said it was only right that you should have it." He paused. "You're the fisherman in the parish, he said . . ." And then Art added, "monsignor."

The priest snorted a little laugh. "Tell your uncle," he said ceremoniously, "that I thank him in the name of the parish." His face assumed a look that was supposed to express the whole parish: it was like a proud pink kite beaming charitably down on the neighborhood. "Father Boris," he muttered, "take the fish," hardly moving his lips because he was hooked now. When the little priest bent under the weight of the pike Art was free at last.

It was only as he came down the last step from the rectory that he realized the fish was gone as suddenly as it had come and again he'd been caught unprepared. It had got away from him after all. Now, for the first time in hours, he was without occupation: an unemployed fish-carrier. Actions and people had supported him like sticks throughout the day, but now there was nothing left to do and no one more to see. All he had left was the liquor that had inflated him like a balloon and now the air was quickly escaping. He could only speculate on what would happen to his pike (or what had been his pike): probably it would be kept in the rectory freezer until one day when the monsignor needed it badly, he and Father Boris would hurry down the steps two at a time to the monsignor's Chrysler, Father Boris trudging behind with a big bass fiddle case, and they'd speed off toward the cathedral. And there was no reason why the fish should stop there. Why shouldn't the bishop keep it in *his* freezer? Bishops had bosses . . . In his mind Art saw the fish going all the way to the Vatican. Who knew what would happen once it was there? Maybe the Pope could work a miracle with it and convert the Jews.

Art walked around the block. Once more he was before the rectory. Looking in at the light on the second floor it occurred to him that he'd been robbed. The pike was gone, and all he was left with was the neighborhood he'd known all his life, the dark houses standing heavily across the street, the church's hulk confronting them like a wall. The black trees rocked softly in the warm night breeze that carried from the corner the sagging, broken music of the juke-box and the voices of merry thieves in the bar. His world was complete again: even the stars above Detroit, that looked like holes punched into the roof of sky, were part of it—just burning coals cooling to ice. Worse still, he knew that soon he'd be sick. A greasy feeling had been filling his throat. (He thought of his hamburger and it didn't make him feel better.) The unpleasant taste of liquor was rising. Soon, he feared, he was going to have to throw up; but there was even some consolation in that. He'd probably have to force it up with his fingers, and he didn't like to think of it; but when it was over, he'd feel better: scraped clean, eyes watering, but alert again, unencumbered; maybe he could once more see things clearly.

Margaret C. Szumowski

About My Cousin

I always pretended that Jan Gratowski,
the most famous editor in Poland, was my
cousin. I tried to imply that I, too,
was a writer of caliber. I'd tell the truth
though it cost me my briefcase, my apartment,
my life. The truth is, he is not

my cousin at all; we just have the same
last name—pure coincidence. I never wrote
about Stashu. I don't know what happened
to his family. He died and that's all—
maybe they made it to Vienna. That's it,

they're enjoying Vienna, all the little
clockmakers' shops, the strudels, the strong
coffee—they're living it up. When anyone
speaks of mines, of miners, I just say how beautiful
the salt church at Valiska is, you must

go to see it soon, isn't it wonderful
that men don't have to work so hard any more,
mines cave in, going underground suffocates
a man,you'll love the way the salt saints
glisten. Get it straight, that famous editor

is not my cousin, and since we joined the party
we're much happier. See my villa, see the soft
bathroom tissue, see the pantry full of
porkchops and potatoes.

Bronislaw

Mother's borsht was steaming red
and delicious that day. She carried in
pierosky, sausage, ham and sauerkraut,
mushrooms and poppyseed cake. Father
was already sampling the cognac and

Donald and Richard were laughing like
mad. Uncle Victor challenged me
to drink schnapps. I couldn't keep up
with him. I was already dizzy when he

started his stories, bald head gleaming,
great nose quivering. Who knows why
that day he told us what they'd kept
secret for twenty years. "Your mother

built mud houses with her bare hands,
drove a combine, nearly lost Ganya
in a blizzard; they scared wolves away
with burning straw stuffed in windows."
Mother cried for the first time

since I started school in the Italian
neighborhood and told her I didn't want
to be Bronislaw any more. "What do you
want to be? Macaroni?" she teased.
Now Victor told his own story

and Donald and Richard were quiet.
"They took my belt, my shoelaces, my gold
ring. They sent me to prison and I
got sick and didn't know I was in hospital,
the burning pipes, the kind of place

where you're afraid to reach out a toe
for fear of scorching it but your head
is icy. When I got well I had the job
of taking temperatures. I knew how hot
men got in that place, what did they do

with all the bodies. One day I looked out
to the carcass of a bombed building
and saw it full of bodies, tossed-in,
sitting-up, flipped-over face down . . .

Once I saw my father. It was mealtime,
another line, another room. I saw him,
lined up for the same fish soup. I tried
to rush up to him; I shouted, 'Father, it's me,'
A door shut between us and that was all."

Now we all cried for what we hadn't known
or asked or imagined. And what
was your father's name?"
"Bronislaw," he answered.

The Trickster

You filled the governess' shoes with frogs
and escaped the gypsy who showed you
her breasts. You hood-winked the Germans
and fled to Latvia without a gun.
When the Russians marched you
across the freezing tundra of Novaya Zemlya
and fed you water soup, you lived
because you knew where to pluck
the wild onion.

Remember how you played chess
in the top bunk when they locked you in
to die. You tricked them
and now you are fooling me.
You slip through my fingers
like cool water. Father,

I pull you back.
Already your bones try to disappear.
Your body is old lace too fine
to be touched.
I want you in the flesh.
I need you like a cushion for my aching
but you are thin enough to pass through
the needle's eye.

I will be your fiercest guard,
make a stout cage
of these arms. I will put flesh on,
steel the will, make heart pound,
hands move. I will be your body:
we will breathe, rise . . . You will not

escape me, old rascal.

Going to Zakopane

"And so Mama divided the potato among the three of us.
We were glad to have anything to eat."
Father always told his potato story on holidays
when there was too much to eat.
But once I went to Poland with him.

He made me touch the border.
"Don't worry," he laughed, "they know
only a crazy person would run East."
He made me ride an enormous horse. I knew
nothing of riding—it was so far to the ground.
For three weeks he left me at a school for the blind.
Then he showed me battlefield after battlefield:

where the Poles stopped the Turks,
where they rode with sabers against tanks.
He showed me little white stones, braids of children's hair,
their toys. He loved the whirling gold angels at Gizycko,
the observatory at Fromberk. "Poles are star-gazers
as well as warriors," he said. He tried to teach me

what every Pole knows, the difference
between good mushrooms and bad mushrooms. In Crakow,
we heard the trumpeter's song that ends
when he is shot in the throat. "The Nazis wanted Crakow
for themselves," Father said. Aunt Magda drove us

all over Poland in her two-cylinder car. We slept
in little apartments. Our relatives
spoke only Polish, ate only garlic. Father started
smoking and drinking and looking at women.
He was 15; I was 60.

At Zakopane, the playground of kings,
Father found the view exhilarating.
I felt too ill to step out
on the icy peak.

Biala Vieza*

Farmers on slow carts carry sweet hay.
This purple-flowering Polish earth.
No Oswiecim here. The forest, the forest.
Lead us further into the forest.

Moss carpet. No mass grave, but violets.
No people naked falling
back into the womb. See, child,
your father lives, carrying wildflowers.

We touch our child's face,
run through Polish forests flowering snow.
Taste the last blueberries. Are they coming?
Soon the snow will cover everything.

Your beard brushes me as branches
brush the wanderer into deep. Lead us further
into forest. I fear sabers. I fear wolves.
Soon the snow will cover everything.

Here is the soft snow. Oaks old
as God. We were born
for forests deep with snow.
Your face and the child's are flowers
of this long journey.

*ancient virgin forest in eastern Poland, a traditional refuge from invaders.

Concert at Chopin's House

The people are waiting, waiting
for a cabbage, a cup of flour.
They look so tired—Krisha, big-bellied
with little Ala struggling
in her arms. But for their guests

they find fresh bread, blueberries,
a glass of tea. New city, Nova Huta,
so far from forest, so far from sea. Inside,
a plant defies gravity, spreads over the wall
like tapestry in a medieval castle. Uncle

Bronislaw is always laughing, always fishing;
everyone says he will die fishing. Today
there is a big salmon for lunch. Three generations
in a tiny apartment, no place to rest. But every
couch becomes a bed: even strangers find rest

here. We see the glacial lake, the virgin
forest. My husband is a bridegroom again,
wildflowers in his hand. Gypsies play violins
in the streets of Gdansk. On Sundays

at Chopin's house something spills over, overflows
from the bungalow into the rosegarden, into the hovering
trees. As we ride back toward Warsaw, children's lips

and hands purple with berries. Today
the opera is full; today the churches
are bursting.

Tad Kielczewski

Four Haikus from Poland

It's autumn in Lodz:
The leaves play Russian Roulette
With all six bullets.

She said "No" to me
In front of police headquarters.
Winter in Warsaw.

The crows caw out loud
Unlike any other place:
Springtime in Krakow.

Summer in Gdansk
Gets gdansker and gdansker.
And then it gets gdark.

Marek Baterowicz

Three Kings

Translated by Victor Contoski

We are nearing the end of the voyage
having already lost a sense of freedom
its golden mean no longer a guide
Probably King Midas conquered it
and only his ass's ears catch the breath of dawn
We do not even know whether we should speak
of all life's events
simple and complex
We forget many things
Any road is good
that leads along shadows
among shadows
and by a shadowy path
What we remember was beaten into our heads in school
in long history lessons
beaten into our heads by chalk and blood
Daily we swallow the host of hope and humility
We bow our foreheads before the priest's mitre
the movement of his lips in our eyes
a knot in our throats
In vain we await King Alexander with his sword
while once more King Sisyphus
has the stone of the world slip from his hands

A History of Religion

Translated by Victor Contoski

In the shadow of the pines
at the grave of Romulus
I look for the sign of ancient hands.
In the eternal city columns of temples
today lift only air.
Obelisks of a dead world point their fingers to the sky.
Only day is born continually from night
there where grass grows exchanging in whispers
the immemorial news of Roman edicts.
In daylight over the steps of the temples
among the ruins cats walk
basking their ancient memory upon the stones.
Plebian cat and patrician cat discuss
the fall of the empire.
On the ruins of the altar of Jove
a four-legged priest stretches lazily
pontifex maximum
calling on subjects to make offerings.
But all cats have walked there for a long time
by their own roads witnessing the new
the lasting religion of the Roman alleys
sun worship

###(Ktoś powiedział)

Translated by Victor Contoski

Someone said that love
is a path
into the unknown

I did not know I could go so far
somewhere with no sign
of your footprints

That Day

Translated by Victor Contoski

Martial law declared in Poland
December 13, 1981

That day
hit you in the face
if you had one.

That day
rinsed your ears
in sweetness and venom
in the national anthem, in Chopin's music
and a volley of orders.

That day
opened your eyes
if you were trying to close them.

###(Mój stary)

Translated by Victor Contoski

My old man, says a mountain woman,
when he gets drunk
takes a newspaper to the stable.
There he reads it to the horse
and laughs his head off.
The horse shifts its weight from hoof to hoof
swishes its tail
and is silent.

Fairy Tale

Translated by Victor Contoski

Beyond the seven gates
beyond the seven hobnails
in the kingdom of the deaf
a fight broke out over the office of stentor
and the voices of the silent played a large role
Blessed be the silent
because they possess the kingdom of the deaf
and conquer tropical paradises
rejoicing in the honor
of gathering coconuts
Underground in the tropical archipelago
like overflowing champagne
bubble volcanos

J. Z. Guzlowski

No Sweet Land

Sarah says
see my little girl

she can read a book
make change for a twenty

tell you what star is what
she doesn't need

school love dolls
she knows winter is hard

beds are soft
pumpkins

grow on vines
she knows

what's useless
the soft spade

the easy turn
maybe in Mississippi

somewhere
the soil is sweet

ready for asparagus
or juicy fruit

but not here
here the ground is clay

more clay than dirt
more spirit than flesh

here, you see a dog
you know he's leaving

A Good Death

You say in time
you'll learn
to listen to the Polonaise
and not hear Sikorski
or Warsaw, the hollow surge
and dust of German tanks,
only Chopin,
his staff of clean notes
and precise legato

Your dreams will be
of crystalled trees
papered gifts
in red half-light,
the smell of warm sheds
and girls drawing milk
from waiting cows.
The snow will fall
and go unnoticed.

Helen Degen Cohen

The Edge of the Field

A View from The Ghetto (or, On Either Side)

Here I stand at the edge of the field,
Before me, wildflowers.
Behind me, dark children,
like myself. In the pure spaces
between knotted wire, far off, I see
bits of clothing fluttering
toward us. Nearer.
Behind me, they are staring, some
go home. Others swallow.
Brushing wildflowers they come
closer, picking up stones.
The sun shines on them.
Mama? I am running, running. Away from
their blue shirts like the sky,
their hair like the wheat,
their mended dresses ripped by sunlight,
spitting, cursing.
Down the curb, around walls.
Day after day.
Until we are gone.
All the dark ones are gone.
They have no one.

SHH---*Listen to the way they talk,*
Mirenka:

   "Where did we live before we lived in the Ghetto, Mama?"

   "Don't you remember? On Stolka Street. Don't you remember
when Uncle Dadu and Aunt Rachel came to visit?"

   "No."

Nobody comes to visit. I can walk from one end of the street to the other now. At one end there is a field and at the other end there is a town. People live in the town, but we don't see them.

"What is a town, Mama?"

"A town is where people live, what else?"

"Mama, will you tell me a story."

"A fairy tale? Oh, I don't remember, Irishya. I don't think I can remember. Do you remember? Don't worry, you will have a book."

"When?"

"When. When we can get it you will have it."

"In Polish?"

"Of course in Polish. But maybe in Russian. I don't know. Don't be impatient, you'll get it."

"Mama? Tickle my foot, here."

"Irenka . . . All right. Don't kick me!"

"Where is Uncle Jacob?"

"What kind of question? Down the street. Why don't you know where is Uncle Jacob?"

"Where is Aunt Vera?"

"Aunt Vera . . . I don't know. I don't know where anybody is . . . Aunt Vera was the most beautiful of the sisters."

"Where is she?"

"Ahh! I don't *know*, Irenka."

"I don't have anything to do."

"You want to draw a picture? I have some more paper, here."

"No."

"Please, Irenka, I don't know what you want."

"I want to go out and play."

"All right, go out and play. But don't stay too long. Find Mirka, but come home soon, and don't play with those, you know, those sick children."

"All right, Mama. I want a newspaper, I want to make a boat. Mama? I want to play with the cards. I want to play House. Let me show you how to play House! Come here. *Please*. All right, you just look. You have to make a tent out of two cards, and you have to stand them up on the rest of the cards, and then pull cards out, here, from the bottom. I'll go first. Look . . . see? The cards didn't fall, so I keep the card. I can pull another one because the house didn't fall. Ooops! Don't worry, I'll make the house again . . . Here . . . now you pull. Pull, Mama!"

"Oh . . . I am too afraid . . . Oh, Irenka, I will make it fall!"

"No, you won't. Just try. *Please*,"

"All right, all right . . . this one! See?!"

"See? You didn't make it fall. I told you!"

"And I can do it again?"

"Yes!"

"Oh, that was very nice. I enjoyed it, but that's enough."

"One more game, just one more, Mama."

"No . . . I don't feel like it, Irishyn."

"One more, one more, that's all "

"All right. One more, that's all."

"I don't know what to do, Mama."

"Go out and play with the children."

"All right. I'm going."

"Go. Go."

"When should I come home?"

"Soon. Go."

"Mama, play one more game with me, just one more?"

"No."

"Is it cold outside?"

"I don't know, Irishya. Just go."

Mama has something to cook; I'm going to play with the children, *those* children, the ones near the puddle. I'm going to go right up to them and say

"Can I play with you?"

"All right," says a big boy, his eyes busy on the water. The mud makes curving lines on the water, like paint mixing, and the top of it shines. He says, "Everybody start here, see? — and we'll see who wins."

"No," I tell him, showing him a wider place, "you should start *here*."

"I think we should start where Simcha wants to start," says a girl with almost blonde hair.

They are getting their boats ready and are not looking at me. If I wasn't fat maybe they would listen to me. The other children down the street are laughing and shouting—they don't look sick to me. I don't think anyone has the Cholera or Whooping Cough. Cholera is a "bad word," like "Psha Krev." They are having a good time and I'm not.

"I have a boat, too."

Nobody answers me.

"I'll get my boat," I say. They look up and then down again at their boats.

"Irenka! Are you back already? Irenka? Are you crying?"

"No. I'm getting my boat."

"Boat? What boat?"

"See?" I show them. "But, Look! Look! Miriam's boat is winning!" they say to each other. Simcha rocks back on the cobblestones and shouts, "Ahh! She won!" He is very surprised. A thin girl with curly black hair and big teeth is laughing too and saying, "I'm going to win this time!" "Oh sure . . ." Simcha says, "sure . . ." talking to himself. He is making a new boat, folding newspaper.

"What if there is no puddle later," I say. They look at me

"Here, you put your boat with the others this time," Simcha says. "I'll wait with mine for the next race."

"Okay," I say. "Now?"

"Now!" he says. Now we all put our boats together, we line them up across the little muddy river, I feel water on my hand and the sun on my head, and we are so excited. "Maybe I'll win!" I say.

"Maybe you won't!" Simcha laughs. I want Simcha to like me but I'm not pretty, like Miriam. But the other girl is ugly. When Mama sees her, she will say, "Look, Irenka, how big her teeth."

"Let's play a game now," I say, "follow me!" They look at me. But they don't follow me. They don't think I am very important. I made an excellent boat. I like making those boats; I could make a hundred boats, it is so exciting making the boats, but I may not win the race. I don't like racing too much.

But they are not looking at the race, they are looking at the soldiers going into a house. They are looking at what will happen. I don't want to look, but I am looking too. The soldiers are taking people out of the houses, by shouting and pushing. I leave the boat race. I hide behind the corner of the house, but I am looking. People are putting their watches and rings into a basket, others are following the soldiers down the street, away into the town. Someone is crying. I am not crying. They are not going to find me. I am smart, I am not like everyone else, I just had a birthday party, Mama put tea and marmalade on the table, and the faces were looking in the window . . .

It is quiet and I pass the children at the puddle who are still looking, but at nothing. I stand next to them, wanting to go home. I don't know why I don't go home. I want to know something, but I am afraid to ask them. Karla, the curly-haired one, says, "My mother went with the soldiers." "Where did she go?" I say. Nobody answers me. "Don't worry," Simcha says, "some will come back—soon. Some always come back." Karla is not saying anything, but out of her eyes water is running. I want to run home, but I can't, just as I couldn't run home from the edge of the field. I can't move. "You have to be very healthy," Miriam says, "you have to have muscles for working, to come back." Karla's eyes are stretched open but she is not moving, she is looking at nothing. I hate Karla. "Muscles, shmuscles," Simcha says, "it makes no difference." A tall girl walks up, listening. "Children are no use," she says. "Who are *you*?" Simcha says to her. "And you," he says to me. I am confused. I am not a stranger. "*My* name is *Irenka*," I insist. "Who said it wasn't." Simcha laughs. I don't understand. Something terrible is going to happen.

Mirka has walked out of our house, and is coming to play with me. "Nothing is going to happen . . . " she sings for everyone, smiling and looking down with black, dreaming eyes, "you are all so silly . . . of course they will come back . . . Come with me, Irenka," she pulls me up, "I want to show you something . . ."

I go with her, but I don't believe her. What if it happens when I am playing cards with Mirka, what if it happens when we are making glass bead rings. Something bad inside of something terrible, inside I am hot, I am so hot I open my mouth to let it out.

"I'm not playing," I tell Mirka. "I'm going home." "Oh . . . you people . . ." she sings, looking around at everybody, still smiling. When I go home I will tell my father that Mirka's father gave her a gold ring. Sometimes my father gives me a ride on his back. Once, he went away, I don't know.

"What! What happened, Irenka?"

Mrs. Katz comes over from behind the hanging sheet, scratching her head. "They took some people to work," she says.

Mama sits down on the bed to stare. I am shaking her, "Mama! Mama! Mama!" She moves her head away from the stare to look at me, but she doesn't see me. I am shaking her, "Mama! Mama!"

Mrs. Katz comes to my mother, shaking her head. "You people . . ." she says like Mirka, "you have no faith. They will come back."

Mama says, "Don't worry, it will be all right." I lie down on the bed. I am going to stop crying soon. "It will be all right," she says, and I'm going to believe her.

But at night they are talking in Yiddish so I won't understand. They call me a *kind*. It means child. I never told them I understand everything.

I am in someone else's house. I have to stay here because Mama and Tata went away for a little while. In the dark they tell me to lie down next to a boy on a cot. I find the cot and lie down. It is very warm next to the boy, and he moves close, he is very soft. I don't know if I am sleeping, but I couldn't see the boy even if I opened my eyes—he is behind me; but I don't want to open my eyes, I move closer to him, and he feels so good, the boy, I can feel his bare leg around me, I can feel the warm thing between his legs, it is impossible to get as close to him as I want. I don't know what I want. It feels so good though, the boy touching my whole back, his leg between mine. The boy is sleeping. I put my hand between my thighs, to make it feel good. The stars are making light in the room . . .

I am standing at the edge of the field. I have a piece of warm crust in my hand and behind me the houses are quiet. There are only a few small children in the street, sitting quietly. I look out at the neverending field, stroked by a wind's breath; the grass goes

down under it, like sweet-smelling hair, and comes up again. I
reach through the wire for a piece of grass and look at it closely,
then feel it with my tongue. It is different from the grass on our
street. I suck on my piece of crust. Something is going to happen.
I look around—nothing is happening—then look back at the field.
The blonde children must be tired of coming, maybe they are
being punished, maybe their mothers told them not to do it. But—
something is coming out of the field, a blue piece of cloth; a girl,
I think. I don't move. I can't be afraid of just one. Is she crying?
They don't cry, the blonde children, and they are never alone. Is
she coming to see *me*? Oh how do I look, I want to see myself.
But I only feel myself, the skin of my face, my arms, my fingers
on the crust of bread, my other hand feeling the loops of my braids
from end to end. She has stopped running and is walking slowly
towards me, wiping her eyes and streaking her face with dirt. She
stops, where she could almost reach me. She is smaller than I
thought, and her hair is like the wheat in the far field, and her
hands keep pulling on her faded blue dress. She has no stones to
throw and she doesn't say anything. She just stands there staring
at me, her face dirty and her dress torn. I must be much older than
she is.

"Did you get whipped?" I say.

*What if I were in her place, Mirenka, staring at me behind the
fence, a Jew . . . from those Bible places with the darkness of God
in them . . . I just swept around the chickens, where in winter
snow falls covering the seeds with diamonds, but today it got
blown around and my mother told me to sweep. I swept and
swept, in the wind. Behind the barn there was a noise. I ran. The
boys chased me and I tore my slip, and I grabbed my wet dress off
the rope where the hammock used to be, and mother called them.
She can't come out, the Jew, she lives in a circle the fence makes,
like the sun. The others throw stones into it. "Did you get whipped?" she says, behind the fence. I wipe my face. Sure I got
whipped, everyone gets whipped. The boys say that in her circle
there is the devil's food, but I think she has sausage and milk. She
bends her head to one side like Babek, our dog, and stares at me.
They don't throw stones, they just stand in a dark group and stare.*

She sleeps in there, the dark one. They even play in there, their dirty games, the boys say. I don't care. I hate washing and feeding and planting and sweeping. I would show her Babek, and my place in the woods. She wouldn't whip me for playing, she is only a little bigger than I am and her braids are circles. Sometimes I draw a circle around my feet and jump in and out. When I look at her, I think about circles and I don't know what to say. The wire in the fence makes your hand bleed. I brought her something; I found it in a drawer where the boys can't look, or Jesus and Mary, and when they were earning their whippings, sitting down in the middle of harvest—So!, Psha-Krev!, she said, you want to eat too?!—cussing and hitting and making faces, I took it out of the drawer, in the dark room, and I hid it in my hand, and I ran, I ran away from my mother's angry apron blowing behind the barn; and I'm going to give it to her, the Jew one. I wouldn't throw stones so they whipped me—it was play, and they still did it, and they whipped me for not doing it, but the stones were too heavy, and I couldn't lift them into the circle of light. They called me a sissy, they cussed. And she saw it . . . my hand stuck in the sun. "Did you get whipped today?" she says. They don't say anything, but they know everything—they have secret eyes. I'm going to get closer. Someone washed her dress and tied up her hair in circles, and she's pink as jam. I remember what's in my hand, glistening like something maybe she's never seen. I'm glad we're children, we're not mothers yet, we don't live in strange places, and I have this to give her: it is a silver cross, which I myself found, and it gleams in the sun as if all the powerful saints had hallowed it . . .

"Did you get punished?" I ask her again.

She doesn't answer. Takes a last slow sob, like a deep breath, and looks around at the field, as if wanting to say, "You'll be sorry, you'll see." She is a funny little girl. "Well? Did you get whipped?" I ask her, excited, because I have never been whipped. I could comb her hair and close her eyes and put her to sleep. I could make her a cup of tea.

She is smiling at me. She has something behind her, but she's shy.

"Mama, there was a girl behind the fence. She was smiling at me."

"A Polish girl?"

"Yes. She was smiling at me."

"That's nice. She must be a good girl."

"I'm going back."

I can't stop staring at the field. Behind me the children are sailing boats, and Mirka is looking down at her gold ring, putting her lips to it, but I must stand here looking at the fields. The bottom of the sky is stretched pink from side to side. The sun hides and now in bluer air the daisies and buttercups fade to whispers in the grass. O the good words, the gentle flowers. Into the misting field a sweetness has fallen, a sparkling like my glass beads. A group of birds, in the shape of a flying bird, is floating across the sky.

"Mama, did you get me the book?"

"Yes."

"What!"

"Here is the book. Hans Christian Andersen."

"Do you like it? Irenka? Do you like it?"

"Don't read the whole book now, save a little for later."

"But you didn't eat!"

"Soon, it is going to happen soon," Tata says to Mama in Yiddish, in the quiet of the night. He has brought me another book. I've had books before. I know all about the Match Girl. But true princesses can save themselves, magic things and people come to help them because they are good. The children don't follow me, and I am such a good leader. If I were whipped like other children I would be good, but my father won't whip me. I can make up the best games and rules but the children will not listen.

"Mama, do you like me?"

"What? You talk like a foolish little girl, you know? Of course I like you. Everybody likes you, don't be silly. You should have seen how you sang and danced, nobody could believe it. When we had company, they gave you a chair to stand on. And once you danced in front of hundreds of people, do you remember?"

"No."

"Why don't you remember! You sang that song from Al Jolson,

the 'Anniversary Waltz' from America, and you danced with your arms—"

"Like this . . .?"

"See, you remember? What do you mean they don't like you; maybe they are not good enough for you."

Not good enough? But Simcha is the best boy in the world. He knows everything, everyone listens to him. Mama doesn't know that I am too fat, she thinks I look good. In my house I look good, but outside, I don't. Look at the flypaper, black with a thousand flies, hanging so still from the middle of the ceiling . . .

"Irenka, you don't look good. And it is late. You should go to bed now."

"I want you to come to bed too, and Tata."

"Soon, soon."

"Where is Tata . . ."

"He'll be here soon."

Good. Now is the warm time, now Mama comes to bed, now Tata comes to bed, and the dark comes under the covers. Mama curls around me, big and warm, I can feel her stomach, I can feel her hair, I want to bury myself in Mama, I want to dig into Mama and feel Tata curled around her. I can't reach him, I can't reach him! I want to sleep in the middle, Mama. I want to smell Tata's hair. I want to sleep on the other side now, Mama. I want you to turn around, Tata. I want more, more. I want to get closer, let me get closer . . .

Everything happens before the beginning, before dawn. How often we have awakened before the sun, to wait for what will happen, for the awful day. We are awakened by the full, correct knowledge of what will happen; how much better not to know what will happen—to be up into the safe night, and then to sleep through dawn. But what we know comes knocking on the door before sunrise, before the sun has awakened to warm us, and we wake into a strange pre-world ghost-lit by a future sun, when the darkness is no longer dark enough, and only the day that must be lived is living before its time. Look, Mirenka,

How often they move out of bed this way to pace in the gray, stony darkness, one at a time, Tata first, Mama next, whispering to each other, sitting down, standing up, walking to the window, to the door, sitting down to tap on the table with their fingers. Around them people are sleeping, so they can't say, this, or that, and their wild looks fly between the walls, fall dead on the table, into walls. I am stretching, I pretend to be just waking up to their pacing in the weird darkness. It is a cold time to be up, a time before God has decided how nice it would be to have earth, light, water, human beings. He knows everything beforehand, and yet he begins it, there is some use to it; and we, like God, know what will happen and yet we rise, to watch it before its time. Time. Time begins when Mama stands up out of bed bewildered, when Tata pulls his timepiece out of his pocket to find the time. Time, time, time!

Why do they have to get up! Why do they rush the time! The Katzes never get up. If anyone knew how strange my parents were they would never play with me.

Karla is sitting on the curb and crying.

"They say stupid things," Mirka warned me off to the side, but I know, I heard what Simcha said. Simcha is different now. He is sitting with his legs crossed, not doing anything. He just says things as if to no one, as if he is letting birds out of his hand, and they are flying everywhere. Everyone listens to Simcha's birds and then they go home. They don't go home like I go home, they know their parents won't save them. They just don't know where else to go. Mirka hates them. "They are so *stupid* . . ." she sings, they weren't *there*, how do *they* know . . ." Her head falls slowly to one side, her black hair oozing down like molasses, as she closes the caves of her eyes, dreaming, her arms around herself. "Mirka, wake up! Wake up!"

But Mirka won't ever wake up, not after days, not after nights. Days and nights come and go, and Mirka won't wake up.

Mirka sits on a doorstep dreaming about her gold ring, the gold watch her father gave her only today, her father whose face is oily, whose eyes roll down dreaming, like Mirka's. She puts her lips on the gold ring, like a small kiss. O please wake up, Mirka, let's play hopscotch, let's unravel our glass bead rings and make new ones. The street is emptier every day, a loneliness sits in it, its head dropped.

Days come and go.

"Simcha went home . . ." Mirka sings, "finally he went home . . ." But, everyone has gone home. From the fields the children come to throw stones, but we are not there. They walk away disappointed. They will say mean things to their parents. They won't do their chores.

Days come and years go.

Look, that little girl with white hair has come back to the fence. She was told that no one was here any longer, but she didn't believe them. She stands at the fence looking for me. Should I go to her? Will she recognize me?

She stands at the edge of the field, smiling. She knew I would come. "You didn't get whipped today?" I say to her. She shakes her head, still smiling. From behind her torn dress she brings out her hands, and in them a little silver chain. For me. She must have found it somewhere. I put two fingertips through the diamond of space between the thorned wire, and between them she places one end of the silver chain. We don't know what to say to each other, so we laugh. And it is so peaceful around us. It is such a fine chain, it makes a little pool of silver.

Look, I still have it. Right here, in my palm.

Helen Degen Cohen

Sing Illinois

How easy it was to write American poems,
to sit in school with the May-windows open
and sing Illinois songs. *O'er the river gently flowing.* . .
To eat soft, white sandwiches, *Illinois, Illinois.* . .
Lose my accent and walk and talk, like
Superman, the American way. We lived in Texas
for a while, and I talked like a Texan.

But there is another, an older someone,
who had burrowed into the center of the earth
and come out at the other side of the world,
and she packed her bags and is sailing my way. . .

Her ship comes closer every decade, every minute,
the air begins to ripple tensely, like an ocean —
sometimes I think she has already been here.
It takes courage to accept her foreignness.
Let us call her a she and a he, both.
Here, off the sea, comes the one I must love,
regardless of what country she was born in.

A Jew is a gypsy bird among gypsies.
How can he belong to any country
when the country he belongs to isn't his?
I was born less in Poland, than I was to my parents
and they to the War, which owned them
like a snakeskin that had left its reason.
And no matter how many places I try on
the new one doesn't fit any better than the old one,
the little one inside, my neanderthal infant
keeps crying Where are we? Who am I?

He carried my books in the popsicle sunlight,
a boy, when I came to Illinois, America.
They bought me a pink robe, a family, I sank
into their sofas—*O'er the river / gently flowing. . .*

But my parents are too powerful a country.
All other countries lie down beside it,
are gardens of prairie and cornfields and flowers,
I live among gentle, deciduous pirates . . . *Illinois, Illinois. . .*
And then, she comes on a ship to remind me,
bearing her gift—astonishment—
comes to subdue me. And I stand up.
Oh, I was ambitious, I wanted to love less
than my true gods.

Light

We live in a prison, Mirenka.
The one called Adam
said, "We'll manage—if the world
were lit with a single candle
we would all live by *that* dim light
and the candle? would become the sun."
But we live in a prison.
When *I'm* free I'll live by
the sun and the moon, not this
lonely beam from the outside
they call "the light of freedom."
Only, to escape, someone
must open the gate for me, and
a guard guards the gate,
a giant drunken guard.
They say that sometimes
I sound like a child—but they
only huddle in the pall of this
prison light. I thought
only prisoners were unhappy, but the guards
drink and are unhappy.
They resent us and are so unhappy.
And they are afraid of us.
The Commandant himself
is a child, who never wanted this job of
running a prison, who schemes now
to save us; and he
is the saddest and dearest bad man
in the whole prison. He actually
let us see him cry. Yes he is the one
who cries. And brings us oranges and Easter eggs.

While the sick lightbulb wanes to the sound of
evening gunfire. Oh evening, the dying
of all light except for this bulb
hanging from the dead center
of the room. In tuberculin light
two black eyes sparkle
and they are the windows.
Those two views of darkness more alive
than the light we live by.

The Prison as a Gray Box

There is something you refuse to recognize:
the guard at the gate is human.
You raised him to be the guard
and he stands there being human.

> *We don't like his stupidity,*
> *his red nose.*

But it's your alcohol that made him drunk.
And the orders he gets are not God's.

> *The problem is how to persuade him*
> *whisper in his ear that*
> *WE own certain passes*
> *and WE are allowed*
> *to just—walk out.*

Your thoughts will make him cheerful.

You refuse to understand him:
he is, above all, responsible, this guard.
He won't hear your fantastic arguments,
as if you would really take him
on the back of your magic bird,
like the one in his bedtime stories.
He knows you want to trick him,
just because he is a little drunk,
because he dreams a little.

How stupid it seems, to be circling
around this dilemma, around and around
the prison yard, as the light dies.
And all because of the bulldog at the gate.
No one else, not a soul, is in sight.
A group of us, say five, could subdue
the idiot among us, regardless of his size.
At leasts it seems seemly to discuss it.

All night the tightening silence
condenses into action—there is not enough time
in the hand of the killer, time compresses
to a weapon forged by the very air, so sharp.
The weapon is brought to his throat, as the guard
laughs unsuspecting, talking about his health,
the way his heart, for instance,
fails him sometimes.

Then there is silence.
Then we are afraid.

I remember coming into Warsaw, a child

out of a sheer, sunlit countryside,
where sometimes a goat made the only sound in
all the universe, and a car engine would certainly
tear the wing of an angel. Entering burnt Warsaw
and the Sound of the World, how strange, how lonely
the separate notes of Everything, lost in a smell of
spent shots still smoking, a ghost of bombs, a silence
of so many voices, the ruined city singing not only
a post-war song but an Everything hymn of dogs wailing,
a car, a horse, a droning plane, a slow, distant
demolition, hammers like rain, the hum, the hum,
bells and levers and voices leveled and absorbed
into the infinite hum in which the ruins
sat empty and low like well-behaved children,
the ruins, their holes, like eyes, secretly open,
passing on either side, as we entered Warsaw, an air
of lost worlds in a smoky sweet light ghosting
and willing their sounding and resounding remains . . . .

In Hiding

For the many days in hiding with a Catholic woman
in a countryside beside a place called war.

Once, in hiding, we went open —
riding in a lenient sleigh
buoyant on the lack of sound and motion
full-away from war
sleepweaving through a back country
my white-haired "lady saint" and I
our frozen faces craning
from the homespun color:
one soft hour the sound of bells was all.
We were missed by the storm
in its silent eye:
mounds of forest meandered past us
and clearer, closer intrusions
fled like calendars behind
their knowledge of our presence —
nature had to wait, we folded leaves
to dream in our escape, the sleigh
was like a god-crib carried by
some fabled beast across her snowy haven
and it hazed the deep green to a waiting green
where animals we knew of kindly
slept unblessed. Our war went still
and deep, around the weightless sleigh.
And in a trembling present,
tense with the lunacy of peace
such as it is, a masquerade in blooming
shades of sacrifice, of comfort jaws
of love-drops like the red of war —
I crane my turtle-head for frozen air,
or burrowing, into
the soft escape, the easy ride,
I hear, beside the child I was,
those solitary
bells of joy pulling
a lonely sleigh . . . .

Anthony Bukoski

Tango of the Bearers of the Dead

W hat did he see that he'd come so often to my house and cup my face in his hands? What was this man looking for who was not my husband? This Frank Kornacki.

At the top of the dresser mirror a plain wooden border forms a scroll with lilies carved around it. As a child I was left to imagine the devil. Below the scroll is my hair, which I have pulled in a knot. It has kept some of its color. Though I am hardly younger than my husband, my skin has stayed soft. My mouth curves down at the corners. When I hold my neck this way or that the loose skin stretches under my chin. No matter how I try to dust and polish them away I see the imperfections of my face, so I try to discourage remembering. I am not grateful to God for my long years. The mirror on the dresser is too honest with me.

I've imagined the devil, wondered at his looks. Once in *Bialy Brzeg* before we came here, my father told me a story. "There was a girl who would not help her mother," he said. "The girl would lie around the cottage. She'd stain her lips with berries, then rise to wash the berry stain from her lips and look in the mirror. Her father and the priest warned her about it, but she couldn't get enough of her beauty. She had desirable eyes. The raspberries stained her cheeks as well. Her old grandmother lived there. Even when the old woman got sick the girl wouldn't help. She gave her time to the mirror — until she saw the devil. She threw the mirror down that morning, cried out, pulled her hair. Each time she look-ed, the devil stared back. Early in the morning, she saw him. At midnight in the firelight's glow, she saw herself and the devil in the mirror. She had spent so much time trying to become pretty that she was being repaid. It never went away. It was there whenever she looked. The devil's lips were as red as her own."

"*Djabel*, demons!" I say and put down the cloth I polish with.

On my knees I pray to the crucifix over the mantel. I beg to be forgiven, to have it as though I was never here and all things about me are forgotten. I see Him reflected in the mirror. The whole room is reflected; its chairs, the cloth that sounds the hour 4 as I kneel, the painting of Jesus on the wall above the crucifix. *O jakie to szczęście moje, że Cię o Boże, zwać moge Ojcem moim, i że Niebo,"* I pray to Him.

My husband lies dying in a bed. Outside I hear my grandson.

"How is he?" I inquire.

"I'm afraid not too good, *Babusia.* Lorraine and Bernice are there. My mother too."

"He's old. He couldn't have gone on long," I say of Antoni Mizinski.

My grandson takes a chair, studies my vase and the oil lamp which has been converted to use electricity. I do not have it on. Without the roselamp's glow there is less to remember. The room has an odd, shadowy peace similar to my garden at sunset. A moment before, I had prayed to be forgotten. It was not my will for life to start. The peonies my husband hand-painted on the lamp's globe grow a delicate green toward the top. The apple tree rubs the window by the mirror where I'd been studying my face and how best it could be forgotten. "He wanted it cut down," I say.

I lay his watch upon the table. Veins rise like knots on my thin hands. "Do you want me to wind it?" I ask my grandson.

"Let me," he says. He takes the key.

"You've never seen it. Your grandfather worked in the car shop of the iron works," I say.

Listening to me, watching me recall my life, Vincent must see my age, my seventy-five ungrateful years. At Christmas we sing *Wśród Nocnej Ciszy* or *Bóg Się Rodzi* and break *opłatki* with each other. At Easter I prepare the food for nieces and nephews and have an egg hunt for the grandchildren. I work in the garden in summer. I want him to see how thin I've become, that I have a hard time hearing, and that listening is a burden to me. My grandson must see I am as frail as the past and not worth coming to visit. I'm not happy when I can be judged. I want no visitors, and yet he is a troublesome one. This grandson, who is already in his thirties and has my daughter's blood, says to me that everywhere he feels the loss of the past. Why should he bother with the past? It's why I've found the black paint in the basement.

My husband's beautiful watch is meant for the vest or trousers pocket; the chain and the key to be kept in another pocket or hung across the vest front. My dying father gave the watch to Antoni—or it was to be a wedding present. My husband Antoni outlived him many, many years and is only dying now.

"Grandmother, I must tell you it's difficult for me to come here," my grandson Vincent says. "Grandpa Tony weighs on me. I haven't any memories of him."

Too late the words escape my lips. "Look at his watch!" I say.

The thin hands point the hours. Between the XII and VI stands a small hand to tell seconds, below that the Russian writing. He sees the tiny figures carved delicately in the silver—the horse's mane, the slight upward curve of the sled's runner blades, the driver's scarf in the wind. He thinks it is a Russian scene. Turning the watch over in his hand, Vincent sees Georges FAVRE Jacat, Locle, ARGENT written in a larger hand.

I tell him that Russians have no ability to make a watch. "The face of a watch, the key, the chain, the vest pocket to put it in, but no inner workings," I say. "They are Swiss."

"I know about my father's side of the family, Grandmother. It's this side that eludes me. I know less about it."

An airplane overhead interrupts our stillness. It crosses for just a second between the sky and the house, casting its shadow on the table. Vincent knows so little about his grandfather because Antoni and I never spoke of our past. For fifty years one thing separated us. We ate together, worshiped, danced, and raised children together, but remained apart. Memory tempered our words.

"Before your great-grandfather Vincenty died he gave the watch to me. It was for my husband, whose dying now bothers you," I say. "Once my husband asked to see the watch. I said I'd show him another time. He knew right off I didn't have it." (I think to myself how Frank Kornacki, who was not my husband, had been gambling and drinking in the town those days. He came here and cupped my face in his hands. He was an embarrassment to me.) "Why did Antoni, my husband, worry about a watch?" I ask my grandson. "When he had time off from work he'd go downtown on the trolley, 'Do you have *Pan* Cieslicki's watch? Was my wife here with it?' he'd ask in stores. One day at the closest store to home where Antoni least thought to look, the jeweler Yano sold it back to him.

It wasn't Yano's fault for keeping it. He didn't know its value when he bought it."

My grandson traces the shadow of the apple tree on the table. "What a bitter story. You didn't pawn it, did you? It wasn't you, Grandmother—"

I don't answer. We sit quietly. After awhile I take the watch and chain from his hands.

"Can you bring out grandfather's violin?" he asks.

He is persistent. He asks me about things I wish to forget. I've watched over him since the cradle. Does he drink or pray? I wonder. How sensitive is he to his wife? Wrinkles on his face betray his years and remind me of my face.

"I used to hear Polish soldiers singing a song," I tell him. "They had no reason to be happy, and they weren't. Now my husband is dying. I was with him this morning in the hospital, but Bernice, my daughter, took me home to rest. I always remember the song 'Tango of the Bearers of the Dead.'"

"Because you think we're bearers of something?"

"Yes, maybe our memories . . . for those who want them. Let's talk about him then, Vincent. Let's say he's here now. Your grandfather, my husband, came right after the turn of the century. We were born in *Bialy Brzeg*, 'White Shores.' There were forests, rivers. He was a Quartermaster in the Russian Army. Have you seen his photograph, Vincent? A Pole in a Russian's uniform, he wears a tunic collar with two scarlet squares. They could tint photographs. Your grandfather, who is dying, went home on furlough once, stayed until it was over, then didn't return to the army. I knew him in *Bialy Brzeg*, but I was already in America. I don't know whether he told anyone he was leaving. He hated the Russians. Like most Poles, he was coming to America to strike it rich. I made him no promises. He played this violin you see before you. He dressed as a musician traveling to fairs and weddings along the border. He had to pay to cross. He had to have money for the train to the sea and for passage over. This part of town was almost all Polish people when he got here. Time has shrouded things, and I can't explain some of them.

"It's like a knot," I tell my grandson. "How do you untie it? Your

Grandfather Antoni built the house. Each day he went to the iron works where he lost three fingers one Friday. If you were hurt on the job back then you were laid off without pay. When you were well enough or hungry enough you came back to work. He cultivated this garden the way our relatives in the old country cultivated theirs. He'd sing a Russian song and kick up his legs off the floor. My husband could do a Kozak dance the way you . . . what do you do now?" I ask him. I've seen too much. I can't look in the mirror without memory. I think of things in the basement.

My grandson follows me to the kitchen where I read the outdoor thermometer. The floral print dress is thin on my arms and back. I pull on a sweater. "I'm chilled," I say.

I take the violin and motion to my grandson. Vincent comes with me down the steps to the backyard. The grass needs cutting. The sun feels good on my shoulders after the house. I lay the violin against the chair, walk a few steps to the trellis. The rich blue clematis has opened out. I retie the knot of twine which holds the vine to the trellis.

"Grandmother Mizinski, come sit down here. We have a pocket watch and a violin."

We sit in chairs in a garden which over the years has become a place of memories I wish to forget. In order to destroy them, I will have to treat the garden with salt, planting it deep in the soil. Vincent has spent much time here with me. I lay the violin on my lap. In places its wood is scuffed or scarred. For years I have cut back raspberry bushes, wishing they were memories. Dreams hang like fragile glass in the air of the garden. They grow out of the fertile earth. Hidden in the twisting grape vines whose leaves obscure the rotting garden posts, hidden in the cool, moist earth turned up by my spade, hidden in shadows of the corn rows; the dreams and memories intoxicate my grandson and make him a lover of the past.

Frank Kornacki was here before with his rude hands. He worked in a hotel, I think to myself. *He lay his heavy hands on my shoulders once when Antoni was bringing in wood. My father couldn't stand this hosteler from Warszawa. I was married. He came again to this house when Antoni was gone to work. Even back then I'd begun forgetting life. Frank Kornacki pulled me to the floor, though I was pregnant. He was a gambler and a drunk.*

"How much do you love me, Róża Mizinski?" Frank Kornacki would ask.

"Very much," I'd say.

"How much?"

He traced the outline of my forehead with hands that held a deck of playing cards all night long. As the clock struck the hour, I would trace the outline of his cheek with my lips.

"How much, Róża?"

"Enough to sell my husband's watch."

When he left I would put the crucifix on the wall again, pray awhile, then prepare Antoni's supper. I'd hum and sing as I did my house chores. I'd sinned, yet managed to look in the mirror on the dresser to run my delicate fingers over the places Frank Kornacki had been. This went on several months when Antoni was away at work.

Antoni and Frank Kornacki. They were acquaintances. One Sunday they gambled and drank in the tavern. Frank Kornacki was losing to my husband. Frank Kornacki said, "Give me the eight dollars back, and I'll tell you something!"

For years after, Antoni kept his faith in spite of the embarrassment. No matter what Frank Kornacki told him, Antoni kept his strength. . .

I tell my grandson, "You grandfather Antoni planted a border of flowers here. Bachelor Buttons, Petunias, pink and white Phlox . . . see how abundantly they grow . . . yellow, scarlet, purple flowers in whose midst you can dance. During dry spells he watered the garden with rain water from the barrel."

"I feel grandfather here, don't you, *Babusia*?" he says.

"It's due to the stories which have been told here and the songs sung or played on the concertina. It's been many years since we brought a radio to the garden. On Saturday evenings a station played obereks and polkas."

I lower my voice and try to forget. Vines, stems, and leaves answer me as the wind shifts. But just like all the other times, the will to remember returns, too strong yet to be abandoned.

I tell Vincent how his Grandfather Antoni Mizinski placed lighted candles on his own grandmother and grandfather's grave in Poland. "In the darkening fields at the end of summer, the goldenrod and caraway brushed his legs, Vincent. From the brittle caraway he pulled the seeds. In the Mountain Ash trees robins ate the red berries, and he always thought the fermenting berries eased the pain of leaving."

"What will I do for my pain in America?" my husband asked me after Frank Kornacki was there.

"How will we get by, Antoni?"

"He forced you down with his hand to your throat, didn't he?"

"Yes, Antoni Mizinski."

"Then I will press that charge."

"But our good name! What will it do?"

Antoni Mizinski, the tears in his eyes, grabbed me, shook me so hard I feared for the baby. . . .

I hear the seaplane and notice the breeze from the lake and the bay. He is dying.

"*Przebóg*, bless me, " I say.

On his bedstand in the hospital is the Polish prayer book, *ANIÓŁ STRÓŻ*, he's had since childhood. The holy card inside says, "If we contemplate the mutual love of Jesus and His Mother, how can we fail to be partners of Their joys?"

"He worked in the iron works and in the chair factory," I say. "He built ninety-two pew boxes for the church in his spare time and as a gift to God. He had three children and farmed for many years. All his life he had a smile for me, Vincent, but what he must have experienced coming over from the old country *and what he must have thought of me. I suppose he held it in. It's true I believe in night terrors and wolves and demons. Where do things go when they're no longer remembered? Do they go far into the depths of some mirrors?* Frank Kornacki—"

"What, grandma?" he asks.

"In the old country we were closer to the days when things might inhabit a mirror, Vincenty. My curious grandson, I want you to forget about all of us who've gone before you. I want you to forget

me and all the things that embarrass a family and make it small.
Bear your dead some other way. I am done remembering."

*Frank Kornacki . . . I sold the watch, and he took the money
for gambling and tobacco, ⅜ of a pound of machorka a week. I
said to him, "Don't smoke. I fear Antoni Mizinski will smell it in
here." Frank Kornacki kept at it. He smiled. "I'm a gambler," he
said and showed me his playing cards.*

"Will you take me to the hospital, Vincent, so I may see him?"
I ask the grandson. The sky has turned purple. He helps me with
my chair and holds my arm up the stairs to the kitchen porch. The
watch and violin I place on the mantelpiece. Even for this late in
summer the wind is cold out of the northern sky.

We pass the abandoned chair factory, the store where Antoni
Mizinski recovered a watch many years ago. The dying fields
stretch out forever to the bay. They were so flat you could see
Frank Kornacki's horse two or three miles away grazing in the
yard behind the house. There was room in this town to walk and
hide in. No one knew but Antoni.

My husband's face is familiar to me, nothing more. His head lies
on a pillow. If memory couldn't interfere, his eyes and lips might be
my own. A part of me would be dying then, not some memory of a
gambler. *But he was different, Antoni. I knew he'd die long before
us. But as far as you were concerned he never died. Even now—*
My husband Antoni looks as he did earlier, and yesterday, and
the day before. Bernice and Lorraine have stepped out to talk
about things. My oldest daughter Gertrude cries out in the
hallway. No change has occurred but the slight bruise on the
hand, which would have held the bow when he played at harvest
weddings. He'd lower his head and left shoulder just at the start
of "Why Did You Come In My Garden?" Then with the first,
sweet notes from the violin, he'd raise his head and smile and smile
at us. He is dying, though, Antoni Mizinski is dying.

Vincent whispers to him. He is the inquisitive one wanting to
remember what I am forgetting. I have no use for the past. One
of my daughters must have combed Antoni's white hair and wiped

his lips. Another old man lies moaning in the bed by the window. Is he as old as I?

"Grandpa Tony," Vincent says.

You, my husband, are so busy. Something holds your attention. You thrash your legs and grow still. What are you concentrating on that your eyes stare so large at the corner of the room? For what reason have you pursed your mouth? Your arms are tied with cloth at the wrist and cloth ties you to the bed frame. It keeps you from moving too violently. The sheets are rumpled. "Let me fix them," I say. *You are safe. Without memories or shadows you have nothing to fear.*

"It is your wife, Róża Mizinski," I whisper.

You stop your wandering to look up, as though you have heard unwelcome news not worth eight dollars. The strength in your fingers works against the knot. Is it the knot of forgiveness? What lies in undoing it, Antoni? No matter how it eludes you, you keep on, my husband of fifty years. I would like to know, does anything matter to you that you persevere, Antoni? You lived, played the violin, raised up our three children, who now make arrangements for you outside the door. Nothing matters to Róża Mizinski anymore, you know.

I say to Vincent, "Sixty years ago he came here with his violin. Over the roads, smiling and waving. Oh, Lord! He told me he prayed and hid from soldiers." *In places rain and wind beat down the grass for you to have a private place to lie unobserved and listen to the wind, to see where you'd be in your journey, to brush aside the goldenrod, to look, Antoni, to the telegraph poles, the orchards, the streams, the paths you'd see tomorrow. I was already here with Frank Kornacki fumbling the laces of my blouse. But I made you no promise. In some places with the wolves crying, you must have feared the night, Antoni. I was waiting in America. Things took care of themselves except that you learned too much for your money. Now there is only a knot left. You try to understand the small knot, the half-inch square knot running over and through itself and tied firmly enough to hold. The hospital is filled with old ones trying to undo these knots.*

Long ago you met me in a Polish garden which was far away

from this bed in the white room. Vincent kisses your hand. "Good-bye, Antoni," he says. *The riddle of our existence annoys you. Let me untie it. Let me undo these laces for you, Frank Kornacki. I want you to feel the child in my belly.*
"*How much do you love me?*" he asked.

It is late. I leave my daughters outside. Some of our grandchildren have arrived in the hall. I begin thinking of the dead in their graves. Vincent drives me home. The priests have told us all along that the dead would rise when the world came to be judged. It is bleak in the fields with the sun going down. I hope you are all right, my husband. "Rest," they told me.

I read the Polish newspaper. I have a quiet supper. Afterward I sit alone in my chair in my part of the house. The phone rings when I don't expect it. "It's about father," Lorraine says. I feel the weather change inside the house.

I go to bed on the night of your death, Antoni. You are gone now. What point is there in staying up? As I pray for you the strangest thoughts trouble me. I am an old woman. The world has changed during our time. We started our journey way before the century. In places in the old days, the wind and lightning forced you to shelter, my husband. You told me you prayed in the candlelight while strange sounds haunted the woods. It was sometime long after planting and sowing, and when caraway was all around you in the fields. You, a journeying man, having prayed to Almighty God, sat and played your violin without fear. You told me, if it were autumn or winter you sat on the river ice. At night on the same River Warta, you said you'd see horsemen with lifted swords come down a valley, mysterious horsemen, Cossacks, Tatars, from whose horses' hooves the sparks flew wildly on the ice, igniting flames in the dry fallen trees along the shore. When you prayed and hugged the violin to you, my husband, when you praised God above and uttered your hopes for me in America, was it worth it? Tell me . . . .

I read your obituary the next morning, the same morning I bring up black paint and a brush from the basement.

Born in 1883, Antoni Mizinski was a city resident employed for many years by the Clyde Iron Works and Webster Chair Factory. Later he farmed in the area. A member of Holy Assumption Church and the Kosciuszko Fraternal Aid Society, he is survived by his wife, three daughters, eight grandchildren, thirty great-grand-children, two great-great grandchildren . . . .

"Good-bye, Antoni," I say. It is mid-September when I throw the last flowers and dirt on your grave.

I try to get my dreams to go away, but they are with me each night for many months, as is common in the season of remember-ing. Until one morning in the dead of winter when terrible storms are threatening, I rise from bed and walk down the cold stairs to the mirror in the living room. The chairs are in place. As the fur-nace hums, the clock sounds the hour. I recall the past. I know where we acquired each item in this room, the doilies on the chair arms, the vase for lilacs and peonies in the spring, the wooden crucifix over the mantel, the painting of the Christ child above that, your prayer book *ANIÓŁ STRÓŻ*, Antoni.

Christ and the devil meet in a mirror. Here you see either His perfect world reflected, or deception, disillusionment, despair. Not having slept so well these past few months, my face is drawn. I will look like this in the coffin. I wear the things of the past; at my throat, the brooch of Grandmother Catherine Cieslicki; around my wrist, the cheap bracelet of Frank Kornacki, a gambler and violator of everything; on my finger, the ring of my deceased husband. In a month or a year I will look like what I see in the mirror this last time, Antoni, a dissolute woman whose hair and eyes I never wish to see again . . . whose lips and throat . . . whose breasts and shoulders I take away from her . . . whose arms, whose old, old body I take away. As I lift the brush over and over the glass of the living room mirror, paint drips patterns on the floor. There is no more remembering God's perfect work. I have no face, no body remains, nothing remains after I paint its refelction . . . this room, this violin, this Russian watch, this pic-ture of Christ. No lamp is reflected here, no table.

Afterwards, after obliterating the memory of my grandmothers and grandfathers, aunts and uncles, Fryderyk in the old country, Brygida, Elżbieta, Jadwiga, I clean the brush of its black paint.

When my grandson visits in the morning, when he ambles through the wind, delighting in the pure, driven snow from the north, no one will be found at home here. All memories will have vanished, all time have stopped.

Kathryn Nocerino

A Governour in Skirts

This is an excerpt from an historical novel based on Edward Cornbury (1661-1723), first cousin to Queen Anne, "whom he resembled mightily." She appointed him royal governor to the provinces of New York & New Jersey in 1722. According to Lewis Morris "he spent half his time in women's cloathing." Supposedly, he also performed official business in a dress. He married Lady Katharine O'Brien and had six children, three of whom lived to adulthood. He served as governor from 1702-08. In 1709 he was arrested and thrown into debtors prison in New York where he spent the following year. In 1710 his father died and he thereupon became third earl of Clarendon, paid off his major colonial debts, and returned to England. While still in New York, he had misappropriated colonial funds (intended for the defense of the colony) and was said to have made deals with pirates, insuring them safe harbor in New York. In addition to all his other habits he was a compulsive gambler and heavy drinker. Upon his return to England, Anne named him Ambassador Extraordinary to Hanover. Some of his New York and New Jersey debts remain unpaid to the present.

The narrator is an Anglicized American Indian educated at Oxford who has faithfully recorded his impressions of the customs and people he found in England.

(These grand dining-halls all possess doors large enough for trees to walk through, and flanked on either side by young men with the stamina to keep upright throughout dinner.) Voices were raised and then the doors flung themselves open. The man who led the household servants—"butlers" is what the English call them—raced in. "A strange woman, Milord . . ." The disturbance behind him grew until someone—whom I took to be the woman in question—burst into the room. She was quite tall—almost the great height of Lady T_____, exquisitely gowned in a pale green watered silk. When she drew away her fan, I saw that she was not attractive. I remember having been struck by the size of her lower lip.

My host, giving forth a peal of laughter, sprang up. "Edward, you fool!" After much back-slapping, he piloted the man—for man it was, on closer observation—to the empty place beside me.

Asked our host, "How does my Lord Cornbury find his escort of the evening?" and indicated me.

Cornbury's eyes—pale blue like those of certain fish, expressionless—I thought, tipsy—and slightly protruding—moved from my braid to my—caught, I fear, within the table-hangings—feet. As I stared back, the image of Uncle Frog visited me. How many years had he spent dressing hides and pounding grain among the women? My Lord opened his fan and fluttered it before his face. "He'll do," he said. Let me hasten to assure you, father—there has never been anything untoward between us—we just happen to find each other amusing.

"And where is the Lady Katharine to-night?" our host inquired.

"France. Or Italy. Or some such place where there are dressmakers." He turned to me. "The poppet is never content with last year's garments. To show oneself to the world in such a manner would mean disgrace; nay, perdition!"

"And let us all guess who makes use of her cast-offs!" said our host.

It was a merry evening, filled with jests, many of which were occasioned by my Lord's presence. He provided a welcome relief from the general run of conversation. Later on, I found that I was actually able to sleep without my customary resort to a swim.

In short order, I was summoned from my rooms at Oxford to squire my Lord about town. As if the sight of a large man in a dress were not sufficiently odd, he wanted me beside him—the ultimate exotic—to ensure notice. You well know what a lover of pranks I am. Alone, or even with Bear, I could not play them. As "savages," everything we did was automatically accepted. "Oh, look, they drink wine out of ear-brasses: how quaint!" Absolutely nothing would shock them; I was near provoked to violence. Now, I suspect that Bear has been painting me as something of an opportunist for "leaving him behind." I am sure that is how he would put it. This is patently untrue. I introduced him to my Lord. Edward's only reaction was, "Mercy, who is this lout?" I am sorry; nothing but the facts will do.

I left Bear glowering in our room and set out to conquer London. Travelling with an English noble is quite an experience: the people deny them nothing. Whenever a thing was given, though, I saw figures being entered in a book. I once enquired about this of Edward: "Are they writing of it in their memoirs?" He chucked me under the chin and called me a foolish boy. I do not like to be considered a half-wit, father—as you may well remember. One of these merchants I took aside and questioned. "I am summing up the bill," he said. "Sooner or later, my Lord will make good."

There is no sense of fellowship among these people, no grasp of hospitality. Were they Kwakiutl, they would burn their very houses down to the bare timbers if they fancied that would please their guests. Alas, England is not like that. Edward and I spent much of our time dodging creditors. They would enter through the front door, we exit through the back, as in an Italian farce. I believe, as I have been taught, in honoring debts. But who knows how it is among strangers? The traveller, in order to clear the path for learning, must keep an open mind.

In the beginning I found my Lord's game of evasion pleasing. With time, however; or, rather, with constant repetition, I began to note that what I had at first taken to be an amusement—one of his many elaborate turns—was nothing of the sort. I still cannot claim to understand it, but here is how I think it operates: there exist two opposing bands. On one side, we have our merchants— some considerable, others yet struggling to establish themselves. They are, with notable exceptions, loud, anxious, and untutored sorts—or so the general opinion would have it. On the opposing side, if I've got this right, are men of quality. These are the guardians of culture and the social graces. By their very existence they provide an example to the peasantry—a benchmark, if you will, toward which the commoner might reasonably aspire. For this service they must be supported by the mass. Those who would raise mere commerce above the necessities of beauty pose a danger to the body politic. One must seize every opportunity to counter them, the running up of catastrophic debts being the most elegant tactic.

During the latter months of my time in England, I began to fear that my Lord was starting to lose ground in his struggle. It is fortunate that others were of like mind. We were dining at court one evening. The Queen was in excellent good humour, having won an enormous sum at cards with Lord S_____. To show you what a great and generous heart she has, Her Majesty is allowing him to play a return game in order to recover his estates.

Perhaps the Queen's good humour was partially owing to the meal. She and her husband are fine eaters; you would be amazed. The English make a ceremony of everything, their meals not excepted. Perhaps their hunger is whetted by the extreme slowness and ritual of the serving process. We simply fill a dipper from the bowl, go off and enjoy it quietly. Here, they must remark on everything—its size, its quality, its rarity, the method of cooking; even the way in which it is served! I must admit that, at first, I found this sinful, but with time have come almost to enjoy it.

This evening, four men were required for the bearing of the centerpiece or "conceit." The chef spends hours arranging of these, the notion being to imitate, with edible components, some form out of nature. The thing was indeed large. The company allows these displays to rest undisturbed for some minutes while they regard their aesthetic qualities. Then they hold a kind of game or competition in which the diners outdo themselves with the splendour of their comments. Please withhold judgment on all this for as long as you can. Take it from my lips: these English are a strange race and must be allowed their quirks. At last, the Duchess of M. (whom the Queen, in the many fervent letters she pens while out of the presence of her consort, addresses as "Mrs. Freeman"), unable to restrain herself, squealed, "This most cunning of foxes is at last trapped for the royal board not by a hunter's wiles but by the kitchen's fatal artifice." And then she sat back and primped, as if awaiting comment.

Signor Cantalupo—these chefs are accorded the honor of receiving applause—at this, turned bright red. He bowed, recovering himself, and marched stiffly out of the room. The Duchess gazed right and left. "La! It would almost seem that I had offended the creature."

Prince George was already gnawing on a bread-loaf. "My dear," he said, between bites. "Tisn't a fox at all. It is meant for a crocodile."

"The posture is very like that of a fox in its burrow," replied the Duchess.

The Queen, who had hitherto played the role of spectator, now commented: "Enough of your nonsense, Sarah: I know my game-animals. If this is a fox, I am a unicorn." Thunderous applause followed this, as it does nearly all of the Queen's rare utterances. You must appreciate, father, that dinners such as the one I am describing occur rarely at St. James', the reasons being two: the Queen's constant indisposition and her utter lack of talk. She cannot manage conversation; it is as simple as that. My Lord Cornbury tells me that she drives her visitors to the point of madness. During public receptions the Queen must speak first, you know: etiquette. My Lord says that as much as fifteen minutes have gone by without so much as a cough out of her. And when she does speak, it is likely to concern the weather. People suppose she favours Mrs. Freeman so greatly for that lady's verbal gifts—the attraction of opposites. Some—basely motivated, no doubt—say that Freeman, on her own part, is constantly bored.

But I stray from my subject—the dinner. Freeman could not, upon hearing the Queen's remark, prevent herself from coloring slightly. At this, Milord leaned over to me and whispered something about "fatal pride." I record it here in the event that the words might some day prove significant.

I do hope I have not misrepresented the Queen's character: she is slow, but by no means stupid. I must allow, however, that the English people, while obeying their rulers, seem to hold them in low respect. Allow me here to reproduce a verse of which the urban rabble are exceeding fond. It began to be sung shortly after the late King William's coronation:

> "King William thinks all,
> Queen Mary talks all,
> Prince George drinks all,
> And Princess Anne eats all."

The English commoner is notably insubordinate. Mr. Defoe, the pamphleteer—who is often in our company—says that his English workers will consume twice as much, and do half the labour of their Dutch counterparts—complaining all the while of the inadequacy of their wages. Most English, on their part, loathe the Dutch as misers—but more on this later.

Let us return to the Queen: you may consider that the only thing a woman knows about game is the cooking of it. Not so with the English—a proviso here—not so for women of their upper classes. They are inordinately, one might say obsessively, devoted to hunting, the Queen being no exception. As a maiden and a young wife she used to hunt on horseback. Since the birth of her son (an unfortunate child in many respects) she has grown so prodigiously large that she now follows the chase in a high, wheeled cart built for herself—a vehicle, to my mind, more like to pitch its rider earthwards than the gentlest of mounts. I should think that a quarter-horse could bear her, but perhaps she thinks it more befitting of royalty to be served by a machine.

I once followed the Queen on such a hunt. That was my first and last sally, for reasons you will presently comprehend. We started out from St. James' of a morning, in full sun. Our destination was one of the few remaining stretches of Crown lands—one among the dwindling group of unsold parcels. Milord tells me that, in his early youth, one could ride all day without coming to the limit of these properties. The hunts, as a result, are not what they used to be. I concluded, at his remark, that the business would be over quickly. I had not, however, kept the resourcefulness of the English nobility in mind. At the rim of the forest, we quickly sighted a deer. The huntsman sounding his horn and the dogs baying, we immediately gave chase. We were out of the woods in minutes and, to my astonishment, had entered onto cultivated land. I started to rein in, but was scolded by my Lord. The deer, the hounds, the huntsman, the beaters, and the rest of the party crossed the field—a patch of vegetable marrows— sending the freeholder and his team of oxen running for safety. It is no wonder to me that the subject of trespass is so often raised in the House of Commons. If the smaller houscholders were allowed free access to game—even that on their own lands—I am sure these protests would moderate. All in all, we went twenty-five miles that day before the deer—exhausted—allowed itself to be brought down.

I am still at dinner, though. The Duchess had turned unusually silent. The Queen and her husband took this as a signal that the meal should begin. Father, I know not which of them is the better eater. That night the main course was a leviathan of roast spring lamb — the centerpiece earlier mentioned. Anne and her husband consumed a prodigious amount, the maids directed to wield the sauce-boats liberally. With this came leeks, turnips, a dish of roasted pigeons, a lamprey pie, and an abundance of brave wine. The two of them were still eyeing the roast, and for a time, the steward was not certain if he should carry it off. At last he did, not without obvious trepidation. Correct as to the Queen's mind, his back absorbed a look of anger from Prince George which, had the poor wretch but noted it, would have shortened his life. On this occasion my Lord Cornbury was sitting to the left of the Queen. For once he was soberly dressed in male clothing. I know not why. Either there had been criticism which had reached the level of court, or everything was with the laundress — I disremember. Edward was trying his best not to stare at the Queen's garment which as he had mentioned early on, was preposterous. "Someone," he said, "has persuaded her that the liberal application of silk bows increases the wearer's daintiness." He blinked fiercely into his claret. "This may be true," he continued, "of a small-boned female, the type who, in her normal garb, looks merely insipid. But" — darting a glance at the Queen — "on a figure of such commanding girth, any indulgence in ornament will serve to magnify." At this I involuntarily looked her way, and was constrained to agree. Signor Cantalupo's "fox," the tatters of which were now being et by the household staff, had been less complicated.

The butt of his criticism was now smacking her lips over dessert — syllabub or Floating Islands or some such thing. I cannot eat of these — they make my teeth hurt. This Edward and I have in common. Give my Lord a pipe of Madeira and he will be perfectly content, although, in truth, he may be over-fond of the stuff. Who am I to criticize, though; just look at our fellows. We drink more, even, than a common Dutchman. Prince George too is famous for his indulgence; also the Queen, but she confines her efforts to toasts and the communion service. Anne is an avid churchwoman.

I once ventured to suggest to my Lord Cornbury that his ruler's illnesses may owe something to her manner of nourishment. "Dr. Radcliffe said as much," he laughed, "and look where that has gotten him!" Radcliffe, if I remember correctly, once attended the Queen while in his cups. When asked later what was amiss, he said 'twas a case of the Vapours. As it is well known that Queens do not get the vapours, he soon found himself without employ. This I thought unfortunate: Radcliffe is one of their few competent practitioners. The one she has now would rather please than cure her, having, in any event, too little skill to accomplish the latter. The morning of the coronation, at breakfast, she called for anchovies. "Nothing salty," said Dr. Radcliffe, "how many times do I have to tell you?" But anchovies it was. She had to be carried to and from the ceremony in a chair.

The Queen is of a placid disposition unless countered. Some think Anne's consort stupid; not so—he is merely of average intellect. It is the contrast between the man and the role into which he has been thrust which make him seem so. If you were here, father, you would surely remind me that, among our nations, leaders are chosen by ability rather than birth—of which I rest painfully aware, thanks to father. The Queen made her first project a campaign to have Prince George appointed High Commander of the military. Anne, you see, felt that he was bored. My Lord Cornbury, however, tells me that this was emphatically not the case. My Lord told me a sad story of Prince George's first months in England. Milord had bagged the job of aide to the Prince—a position, Edward hastened to explain, without responsibilities. One of his few tasks was to write from dictation when the Prince was too fatigued to use his quill. The Prince had had a full day—up at dawn to inspect the troops for William, who was ailing; a reception at Westminster; a tea at St. James'. And it was not much past mid-day. "We talk here," the Prince began, addressing the relations in Denmark who had arranged his marriage, ". . . of going to Windsor, and everything else except sitting . . . which is the height of my ambition." As if this weren't damaging enough, he closed, "God send me a quiet life somewhere . . . " My Lord Cornbury, whatever his other virtues, is not noted for discretion.

I stray from my subject: back to dinner. Sarah, having recovered her voice, was complaining about the health of the Queen's overseas possessions. I did not immediately give this my attention, even when she mentioned the case of "New York." After she treated of a number of other particulars, notably the drop in deliveries of beaver pelts, I realized what she was discussing. Twas naught but that worthless stretch of Mohawk land—narrow, thin of soil, half-denuded by spring burns. I suppose, however, that to these English it is Paradise.

"Fletcher and Bellomont were problems enough," she was saying. "Now that we have removed the brigand Kidd, there would seem no block to greater revenue."

"Ripe for the picking," muttered Prince George.

"Indeed," the Duchess continued, "a man who is full of adventure and wishes to make—or mend—his fortunes . . . "

Milord's shoulders began to quake with laughter: "S'truth!" he whispered, bending toward me, "the wretch who would prefer this job of work must indeed be sorely pressed; I hear the colony is a nest of vipers."

"That bad indeed?" said I. Milord winked.

The Queen looked up from her plate. "Edward," she said, "this seems a perfect living for you!" The Duchess appeared stricken; no less so, however, than Milord Cornbury whose complexion had, chameleon-like, begun to take on the hue of his favorite dress. He forced a smile. "Please! Don't think of it! I am not worthy of this honour. Besides, her grace the Duchess . . ."

"Her grace the Duchess," said the Queen, "has not the ability to distribute jobs." She gazed at the woman. Something has happened between them, thought I: the look, did it carry its own temperature, would have coated the lady's skin with ice.

Edward, however, was too busy biting his nails to remark this. "Really," said he, "I know next to nothing about the colonies." The Queen purpled, "Are there no books?" she shouted in a voice which near rattled the plates.

The Prince who, if the truth be known, half sleeps through most dinners, had been toying with a morsel of stewed plum. The Queen's remark rousing him, he muttered, "Books aplenty. I read 'em all. Wonderful place, the colonies." He looked up, blinking like a burrowing creature which has just surfaced into the light of day. "As Captain Smith put it, you have but to lie under a tree, mouth agape, for the fruit to deliver itself."

Marlborough, the Duchess' husband, here interposed: "True, the lands are rich; however, the French being so close, in Canada, any Governor must needs be skilled in military . . ."

"Edward was the first officer to come over to the Protestant side," his cousin Anne remarked, "for which we shall always be grateful." Let me add here that the Popish side was none other than the Queen's father.

My Lord smiled. "A little game of draughts?" he asked.

"Edward," said the Queen, "we are discussing your future!"

"Your Majesty," breathed the Duke, "may I respectfully suggest . . ."

I thought for a moment that the Queen would expire. She drew in her breath and seemed to swell up, growing redder by the minute. "You and your little wife think you have me well figured, do you not?"

The Duke recoiled: "Your Majesty," said he in a fainter than usual voice, "we think nothing of the sort. If you will permit . . ."

"You have my permission, John, to be quiet."

Edward sat watching these exchanges. Fear had rendered him unable to speak. I thought of interceding but—who am I to them? Who indeed. If Edward's opinions held no weight, how would mine be received?

The Queen, composing herself, now produced the loveliest of smiles. Gad, thought I, my poor friend is truly in for it. "Edward," she said, "will you or won't you accept the job?"

Edward looked like someone from whom the doctor has forgotten to remove his leech. "Cela va sans dire," he said, executing an absurd seated bow. "How could I refuse?"

"Well, that's that!" said the Queen, and rapped on the table with her closed fan. "Blodgett, fetch the dice!"

Danuta Vidali

Sogno di mi Stessa Come Pesce

Da due lenze ero attratta.
Piantato nelle mie branchie un amo
sapeva già il loro danno.
Lo sterno arcato come arpa,
nuotavo verso tutt'e due
in un'acqua tiepida e ossidata.
Mentre nuotavo la rugine è diventata rossa.
Non vedevo più le lenze.
Dentro il sogno il sogno
era già finito.
E io già cotta ero diventata
rosso ardente dentro un cuore
che non era mio.

Dream of Myself as a Fish

Two lines drew me.
A deep hook in my gills already knew
their harm.
In warm rusty water I swam
towards both, my sternum bowing
like a harp.
As I swam the rust turned red.
I could no longer see the lines.
Within the dream the dream
was done.
I was already cooked,
and had become red-hot
in a heart that was not
my own.

Translated from the Italian by Magda Bogin

Danuta Vidali

Solidarieta all'Ora di Cena

A quest'ora le zie polacche
staranno preparando le patate
mentre ch'io mescolo la pasta,
tubero di un passato diverso.
Vedo le mani della mamma morta
che pettina la terra in cerca di radici
per le sorelle.
Lei ci sta dentro quella terra.
Manda su delle patate
come prima mandava soldi à casa.
E sempre stata instancabile.
Ma ogni tanto si ferma
in quel campo di zolle,
si spiana il grembiale,
e si alza per sentire il rumore
della vita nuova
che in alto bolle.

Solidarity at Dinner Time

My Polish aunts
must be cooking potatoes now
while I stand here stirring pasta,
tuber of a different past.
I see my dead mother's hands
comb the earth for roots
to keep her sisters fed.
She is in that soil.
She sends potatoes up
the way she sent money home before.
She's always worked incessantly.
Only once in a while she stoops
in her field of dirt,
smoothes her earthen apron out,
and hitches herself up
to catch the sound
of new life boiling
above.

Translated from the Italian by Magda Bogin

Magda Bogin

Don't Cry for Me, Argentina

T he woman with the little dog goes to Argentina to lose weight. She owns the wool shop up the street. She's married to a short, skinny little guy who sells stereos on 42nd Street and she's having an affair with a singer. How do I know? Look, I'm unemployed, I've got time on my hands. I get a kick out of trying to put two and two together to make five. I'm not talking about how to make ends meet on coupons or food stamps. I'm talking about stories—what makes them hang together. Because every life is a story: good or bad, it has to add up. I guess you could say I have a knack for shaking out what counts.

I usually start with whatever I've got, and before you know it one thing leads to another. Now you take a woman that fat and you find out she goes head over heels for anything petite: toy poodles, needlework, runty men. Right away you're in great shape, because you've got two things: a string of facts and the law governing her life—the law of opposites. Believe me, it's not always so easy, because a lot of times just figuring out the law of someone's life can take you months. Especially since not all fat people think small. Some wear big clothes, drive big cars and hook up with someone fat. Some are half and half. But this one's a total pushover for anything undersize. She's got her life set up so that the only time she has to see something big is when she looks in the mirror. The rest of the time she's pulling the wool over her eyes.

Don't laugh: nine times out of ten a person's occupation is a dead give-away. We're all running away from something. You know what I used to do before I lost my job? Sell furniture—and I'm the product of a broken home. See what I mean? And before that I was a waitress. Same thing. There's no telling what it's going to be. Sometimes the connections are a little tricky—but believe me, they're always there.

With a few exceptions, humanity basically divides right down the middle—into those who go for the same and those who gravitate to the opposite (I'm just telling you what I've observed). Now with this particular lady we have someone on the far side of heavy who doesn't want to know about it, right? Well that may not tell *her* much, but it tells me a lot in a hurry. Namely, that the woman has no intention of losing weight. Keep this in mind, because no matter what she may say or do—diet, spas, meditate, you name it, whatever she thinks she's doing to supposedly get thin—the last thing in the world that woman wants is to change. How do I know? Simple: she's got too much invested in her size. First of all, she's got the dog: one of those pedigreed mutts that fit in a teacup. Right there you're looking at five hundred bucks. Next item: talk about an entire two-bedroom apartment filled with miniature spoons. Maid told me: thousands of dollars worth. And now we come to the real item: that wool store. She and her husband are up to here in debt because of opening that store. Not that I begrudge her the right to knit her heart out if that's what she wants to do: it's a free country. But you don't have to own the place to make yourself a sweater every now and then—or even to pull the wool over your eyes. You can buy good wool at Woolworths. Sweaters too. So you have to look at it strategically. What's she telling herself? In other words, what's the *story* behind the store? Get it? Any amateur Freud can tell you wool stands for femininity (who among us doesn't knit—right, ladies?). So what we're really looking at here is a business that requires her to place bulk orders for a substance she believes she lacks. To repeat, femininity. A stockroom full of wool also puts one hell of a warm cushion between her and reality. But take it one step further and you're really talking. The loan her husband signed to start the business keeps him wrapped around her little finger. He's in deep; her wool trade has to thrive. The reason she's in wool to begin with is so she can stay fat. He likes her fat. So she's got it made. Lose weight and it all starts to unravel.

So far so good. By this point in the game I usually feel a little surge of pride. But since pride goeth before a fall, I try not to let it go to my head. Because now comes the hard part. What does she need the singer for, and why go all the way to Argentina when you can lose weight in the Poconos?

Complicated as it may sound, experience tells me the answer will be simple. Left to its own devices, a life tends to fall apart. That's why most people spend their best years propping up mistakes they've already made. Now it's all well and good to have a husband, don't get me wrong. But once you've tied the knot, to coin a phrase, you have your work cut out for you, unless you happen to be rich enough to live without a man, which most of us aren't. So here's the rub: what's a girl to do if the man she marries, love her as he may, turns out to be a crashing bore but it's *his* money that's keeping her in business? Can she afford to quit? Not our heroine. No way. As we've already seen, she's got too much at stake. She's fast enough on the uptake to know that she needs a lover to hang onto if she wants to hang onto her marriage, which is what's, so to speak, keeping her in wool. Which we've already seen she needs to pull over her eyes.

Now keep in mind that the woman with the little dog is governed by the law of opposites, because that law is going to apply right down the line. So when the demand for an affair rears its little head, this woman's brain does a fast tango with the facts: it asks itself for the opposite of a short, skinny man who sells stereos. Everybody knows the human mind is no different from a computer, which means it will automatically come up with all possible answers to a given question, like it or not. In this case it spits out: a tall fat man who sells tape recorders (machines that take in music instead of giving it out), a tall fat man who sells washing machines (machines that spin but don't make music), and a tall fat man who actually *makes* music. Voila our singer, who happens to arrive on the scene before either of the salesmen has a chance to stick his pointy shoes in the door, and who could just as well have played the violin if his parents hadn't had a passion for Caruso. One slight adjustment: can he be fat? Absolutely not. A fat singer might be the opposite of her husband, but he would be too much like herself. So she goes for a skinny one. And gets him. As I said, the law of opposites reigns supreme.

Now I wouldn't blame you for wondering why the short skinny stereo salesman and the tall thin singer both fall for the fat knitter with the miniature poodle, when millions of lovely women like ourselves are still waiting in the wings. Good question, but once again the answer is simple, though we don't have time to go into it here. You see, each and every one of us has a story line, just as each and every life has its underlying law. I can't prove it, but instinct tells me both these men are governed by the law of opposites. In other words, destiny has put a fat woman in their path. I don't have to tell you that's a whole story in itself, but if we start in on theirs we'll lose the thread of ours.

Which brings us to Argentina. Or, at any rate, the question of Argentina. Talk about opposites. What could be worse than snow in June and torture all year round? That's Argentina. If you look on a map you'll see how far away it is, smack on the other end of the equator and practically impaled on the South Pole. And if you call any human rights group they'll tell you how bad things are down there. Believe me, it's a far cry from the USA. Exactly. Now what did I say about the law of opposites? Listen closely. You and I may think our friend has got it made, but remember, we're living in a world where beautiful is thin. It only stands to reason, doesn't it, that underneath it all our heroine is just like you and me: she wants to be thin. (She wants to be fat more, but only you and I know that.) By the same token, it stands to reason that her husband and her lover also want her to be thin. (They want her to be fat more, but only you and I know *that.*) Therefore, for everybody's sake, including her own, she has to try to lose some weight—and she has to fail. If she tried in Pennsylvania she could fail and keep going back, with the risk of one day succeeding (and thus losing her husband, her lover, and her wool). If she tries and fails in Argentina, she gets a lot more credit and it's harder to go back so fast, because it costs too much. So when an article appears describing Argentina's pioneering use of hunger to control obesity—as well as other ills—she's off and running.

From what I've heard she goes there once a year and loses twenty pounds. She gains them back as soon as she comes home, but she must be doing something right, becase she's still got her husband, her lover, her miniature poodle and enough wool to keep the Falklands warm till kingdom come. Looks like everyone is happy. Isn't that what stories are about?

Linda Back McKay

I Wear My WOJB Radio Cap with the Feather to Embarrass the Children

You fat nursing babies rocking in my chair with me
were happy enough to be crochet bonnetted
in sausage finger productions of tangled hours.
Happy enough to pee in my lap, drool on my silk blouse
walk first steps in my direction
dump bumped heads, loose teeth, sore souls in my lap.

You children wear long black robes
adolescent curls gone grey under powdered wigs.
You eagle eye my thinking, the length of my nails,
my time in the bathroom.
Your handed down opinions
are scapular medals to the pagans.

> I will not part with my bowling shirt
> flamingo earrings, peek-a-boo bra
> even if *the outfit doesn't work, Mom.*
> I will show wedding pictures to everyone
> I will have the biggest bedroom
> I will leave my shoes by the door
> I will be a witch on Halloween
> I will ride the motorcycle
> I will continue to ask what's wrong
> it must be something tell me and you'll feel better.

You should have seen my mother
who loved to dance
wrestle with the wringer for each soapy diaper
rupture cobwebs with the dust mop
dodge splatters over a frypan of pork chops.

My mother, young enough to dance
with a girl, bent herself
over flat leaf plants
with baby brother in the buggy
row by row.
My mother, each pincurl
so tight like curlys on pea plants
face round and red in a turban tied scarf
arms vegetable stained to the elbows
stuffed wide-mouth jars with massive cukes
in great clouds of sweaty steam.

Barely a generation away
I ate pickles on the patio
I tap danced on cracked cement
new as dawn, fuschia
alone with bangs and breasts
horribly big for my age
I watched the egret
that trailed long and white above our house
turn, dip a sculptured wing
and shit purple all over our sidewalk.

Social Blunder

Time was,
moon twirled playing
ring around a rosey
moving tides and poets
touching lovers.
Time was, moon stayed up late
toying with ideas
smiling at sunrise.
New moon runs
with the jet set;
celestial fleshpots
whirling lurid tails.
New moon shuns
eau de earth this season
sneers at comets,
New moon, dressed to kill
hangs with the hoi poloi
pooh-poohs apple pie
eats astronauts for breakfast.

Paul Milenski

Son of Soldier

verybody in the whole house they were speaking in Polish. In the bedroom little Stanley and Mother of Stanley were all of the time making hugs with each other. In the kitchen Old Dziadziu was rocking in his chair and stoking the stove; Old Babci was cooking kluski and pierogi in big pots, stirring with wooden spoons.

But it was being in the living room where the warmth was creeping along the rug that there were being crucifixes and pictures of saints and of Jesus. So in the evening, it was being there that Old Babci was calling everyone to say their prayers.

Mother of Stanley had been saying to him that near to the picture of Jesus was being a picture of Father of Stanley. Mother of Stanley was asking him to pray to Jesus for the safety of his father. So Stanley in praying was always kneeling like Old Dziadziu, with his back being stiff, folding his hands, bowing his head. He was saying, "Boża, Boża, Boża, Amen, Amen." Everybody was smiling to him when he was doing this. Mother of Stanley was saying to him, "Bardzo dobry, Stasiu," very good, Stanley. Mother of Stanley was knowing that he was praying to Jesus for the safety of his father.

On one day in the house, Mother of Stanley was hurrying back and forth, putting colors on her face, taking pins out of her hair, praying, "Oh Jesus, Jesus!" Old Babci she was helping her in finding things. Old Dziadziu he was sitting near to the stove, looking out of the window. When Mother of Stanley was finishing with herself, she was going ahead and putting clothes on Stanley. He was having a tight collar with his clothes so he was sometimes having to move around his neck. Before he was leaving the house, Old Babci was tucking in his shirt, and Old Dziadziu was turning away from the window and touching his hair.

Mother of Stanley was taking him upstreet to meet the bus. They were riding. Stanley was looking at the floor and at all the shoes. The bus was making a funny smell.

Then off of the bus there was being a train station. In the beginning it was looking very big and hollow, but in a while lots of different people were being there. The men were being bigger than Old Dziadziu. The women were having bright red lips, clothes with big shoulders, funny shoes with their toes sticking out. They were having painted toenails.

All at once, everybody was moving to the platform near to the tracks, and Mother of Stanley was saying that a train was coming. She was saying this even when Stanley was seeing that a train was coming. The train was being dark and loud and cindery. It was making the platform shake. It was steaming. Stanley was covering his ears and was feeling like his mother was not really being with him.

From the train the steps were coming down. Big men with all colored clothes and funny hats were filling the platform. The women were running to the men, grabbing them. Kissing them. Crying.

Mother of Stanley was looking up and down the whole train. On her face she was having big eyes and moving lips. Her hand it was shaking.

Then Mother of Stanley was letting go of him and running to a big man. The man was being all in brown with pins on his chest and stripes on his chest. He was being bigger than Old Dziadziu and bigger than everybody else. His hair was being curly like Stanley's hair. He was seeing Mother of Stanley and smiling very wide. He was being: Jesus.

Mother of Stanley was then making hugs with Jesus, touching her hands to his hair, looking up to him, putting her face to his face, over and over. She was kissing him.

During all of the time of this, Jesus was smiling and Mother of Stanley was not turning back to be looking at Stanley. Stanley was feeling that she was not being with him at all any more. His stomach was feeling hurt. His eyes were feeling hurt.

After a long while, Mother of Stanley was saying to him. "Oh, Jesus, Stasiu." She was having tears running from her eyes. "To jest twój tatuś." Jesus, Stanley, this is your father, she was saying.

Jesus was then coming over to Stanley and picking him up. He was having hard hands and strong arms. Stanley was being held higher than he was being held when Old Dziadziu was picking him up. Why was Mother of Stanley letting Jesus do this? Was Jesus going to be dropping him? Was Jesus going to be throwing him like Old Babci was throwing Pootsie, the cat, onto the porch? Jesus was turning him around so that he was feeling that his arms and legs were being somewhere else. He was trying to be turning to his mother but Jesus was being too strong for him. He was only seeing her out of the corner of his eye. She was going into her pocket-book, finding her hankie, wiping her eyes where Jesus was making her cry.

So Stanley could not be letting all of this happen. No. He was making his lips tight on his face. And he was making himself be crying. Very loud. With no real breaths coming back to him.

Jesus was quickly saying something not in Polish: "Damn, I've gone and scared the kid!" he was saying.

Mother of Stanley then was taking him from Jesus. She was saying, "Oh Stasiu, Stasiu, moj kochanusz." My dear Stanley. But he was seeing that she was smiling about this. Somehow his crying was being a funny thing to her. But he was not wanting her to be smiling. He was wrapping himself around her, holding onto her softness, pushing his nose into her hair where her smell was being nice.

And so this is the way they were moving off the platform when all of a sudden Jesus was being back. He was putting his arm around Stanley and Mother of Stanley looking to be proud to be with them. But Stanley was wanting most to be looking proud to be with his mother so he was thinking he would be kicking the arm of Jesus. He was wanting to be kicking but was feeling maybe he should not be doing this. He was remembering about Old Dziadziu instead, thinking how he was always talking in that dirty swear when things were being too much for him all around and making him angry. If Old Dziadziu could be talking this, then this might be something Stanley could be talking.

"Psia krew holera!" Stanley was just going ahead and talking very loud like Old Dziadziu. This was being the way he was always doing it. Dogs blood, to hell!

At this, Jesus was taking his arm away, but it was looking like he was not taking his arm away not to be proud anymore; he was just being surprised looking.

Not in Polish, Jesus was saying, "What did the kid just say?" He was talking to Mother of Stanley. "Did I hear him right?" Then as fast as he was saying this, he was wanting to be holding back a heavy laugh.

Mother of Stanley, after looking at Stanley with big eyes and open mouth, also was holding back a laugh and beginning to jiggle. She was all of a sudden not being able to hold him and was setting him down. The two of them, Mother of Stanley and Jesus, were looking to each other to be laughing some more like before.

"He's learned a lot while I was gone," Jesus was saying, in his laughing, not looking like he was meaning to be saying this exactly.

Mother of Stanley was hunching her shoulders and putting her hands upside down in the air. She was almost losing her breath and taking one funny slap at Jesus. Or was she holding onto his arm? Jesus was liking this. Everything was being so funny.

Then they were kissing again, the two of them, all over like they were kissing before.

To Stanley all this was silly. Jesus and Mother of Stanley being foolish with themselves. There was being a can on the ground and Stanley was seeing it. He was thinking he was going to be kicking the can. This way he would never be going crazy himself over something as silly as finding Jesus.

He was being sure, even as he was moving to the can, that he was not ever going to be praying in the evening in the living room. Not for the safety of Jesus, Father of Stanley. Not at all. Anymore. Because if Mother of Stanley was going to be taking Jesus home to be making him proud, what a dumb idea this was going to be.

Edward Kleinschmidt

Twelve Darknesses for My Father

One day the underwater currents
Won't bring your clean clothes
To shore, there will be no
Shore left, You'll die.
*

But you'll continue to
Walk to work anyway, your
Mind set in snow, blackened
Like the trunk of a winter elm.
*

You will hose off your red car
And the water will blind you,
A neighbor will bring you to
Your back door, and you'll want
To take the house apart, nail
By nail, board by board.
*

As a child you will be watching your
Sisters dress for church, impressed
By the nylon light and the dark
In the folds of the silk blouses.
*

Shooting, drowning
Yourself is no way out.
*

You discover the neighbor with
No tongue, hanging in his garage,
A thick-linked chain around his neck.
*

The men at work move in undertones,
No color on their palettes, they're
Sketched out, outlined, you watch them,
White wooden dolls on the workbench.
*

Half-asleep, you drive the horses, with
Loads of firewood, across the thick ice,
Sell on corners, shout to keep warm.
*

Black gloved fist in your face,
That's all you know.
*

Show me again the gravestone
You bought used, half-price.
*

Remember the buzz saw that sliced your
Fingers and your mother sewing them back on.
*

In December you fade into the snow
Again, you take all the darkness with you.

Red Telephone Near the Davenport

Hot and the wind is not acting
Funny this afternoon. All day on

The telephone, I'm near dial tone deaf
Now, shouting at the strange people

Of Montana, at the sunken voices of
Arkansas, whoever crashed this party

Line, this tin can connected to the playhouse
Out back. My sister keeps shampooing her

Lemon white hair, my parents listen to the hog
Report on the radio—it is Minnesota and summer and

Muggy and I need a shirt to sit on the prickly
Davenport of my dead grandmother, calling out, job-

Less, wanting oysters of love in this landlocked town.
Tonight while everyone is playing cards in the kitchen,

I will sneak off and sit romantically in a country-
Western bar and sip a beer. The waitresses will

Be too busy to ask me to dance. The band
Will be as bad as it can. A change won't

Come over me slowly. The band thumps, a crowd
Forms for five, maybe ten minutes on the dance floor.

Recycle

Every day I say that the last day coming
Around again is gaining. Not overtaking,
But over-reaching, like the Encyclopedia Sale.
Fallow fields are always next in line
For cultivation. Soon the colonists arrive,
Inhabit the hell out of the soil, with
Their reinvented wheels. There'll come a time,
There'll come a time. Right now the helmsmen
Seem oddly overwhelmed, washed overboard.
The cyclamen out front are waving their red
Ripped flags. Draw a line at the point of no return:
I'll be there, high on the list, or low-down,
Somersaulting, pedalling like mad, looking forward.

Possibilities of Love

We are left open and wet like shells young
Girls string on strips of kelp and wear
Around their necks and wrists and ankles into

The sea. In the washed-over sand, we
Have to imagine our names were there, in
Silver, your name like a rabbit, like

Your feet, that turn away from me after
Dark nights soften our bodies, turn
Them into deep pools of water, fresh water

Cupped in our hands on these hot beaches,
The sun which hardens us, our hair
Like field straw, but it is our soft grass,

We nest in it and each other. And our hands
Keep building, like a stonemason sleeping: his
Buildings he has never been in want his hands

Again. It is you I want again, left open.
Now somewhere else, out of reach of my brown feet,
My shell that has escaped into love, my name.

And you are here, now with pearls in your
Hair, and I want to dive to find you
And carry your pearls up to air between

My lips. And to hear you breathe in
As if you were breathing for the world
And will never stop. I sleep on a dune

As if on an animal waiting to carry me down
These beaches to you. And I cannot think of
A letter that is not in your name. And I cannot

Think of your arms without my own wet and
Stretching out. And I cannot dream of your eyes,
Without them, right now, looking closely into mine.

Ed Ochester

Poem on His 44th Birthday

After so many years I've discovered
what my family taught me, they
who never saw gill-over-the-ground
or at least could not name it.
My mother was thinking in the typing pool:
be like those cheerful leaves;
no matter how often you pull
or slash it the foot of its root
will venture out. In drought it
sends its small purple flowers up.
My uncle with his acid stained hands
and eaten-out sweaters must have known
driving the battery truck:
wait long enough and the stripmine will flower,
the birds will pass over and the dock plant
will root, the acid leach out
through the growing humus and grasses.
This must be why they kept flowers
in the gray house, and the dusty ivy
and indestructible snakeplants
which fried and seethed on the radiators.
Even my father, whose heart exploded
between two giant spruce he'd planted
with his pale hands years ago
must have known it, going down,
as he fell for the last time
to the earth and his fingers clawed in,
and the birds whose names he never knew
finally settled and continued
their only and endless song:
rejoice, rejoice.

Cooking

Peel the shrimp, cut the bak choi
on the bias, shred the peppers.
If you wipe the mushrooms
I'll slice them with the chef's knife,
cut the pale breast of chicken into matchsticks,
the mild onion into rings,
start the oil smoking in the pan;
sesame oil is better,
but you can use safflower.

I love you.
And I'm gabbling & cutting
because I think you're happy, too.
Give me a plate. I'll pour wine,
the hell with the thin glasses,
a cup will do.

When I was young I was tonguetied
and I can't remember when the men
in my family
didn't sit, stare at their plates
and shovel, silent as though they'd learned
they'd just contracted syphilis.
And the women, who cooked for love,
beamed.

I think that's why I learned to cook,
so my hands would have something to do.
It's not that they didn't have words,
it's that they didn't trust them.
I mean my hands, and my fathers and uncles.
They never read *Gatsby*, but they believed in him.
They wanted to make money, to take their rich shirts
out of the drawer and spill them across the bed
so someone would say, "what beautiful,
what beautiful shirts." It was cleaner
than talking, or cooking, if you could never
say anything gracefully.

So I learned to love steamy windows, and
I can cook better than my mother.
I can talk better than my father.
And I've always loved pouring wine,
twist it off neatly, or if there's nothing better
put a big jug of Gallo on my shoulder
and without spilling a drop
glug out shots in a cup.
I like my voice and hands.
Over dinner, they meet your hands.

For the Margrave of Brandenburg

When I'm driving up Bellefield in spring
with the window down and Bach needling
the air, Bach at the celestial sewing machine,
as the magnolia petals fall to the pavement
like fleshy coins, I think of you, and your daughters
if you had any—and you must have had them,
any uncle of the King of Prussia must have had
dozens of little dumplings, dressed in silk,
and sons, all pimply in wigs, dabbling at harpsichords,
and not getting it right, poor things—
when the gift of the concerti first arrived
from Bach at Anhalt-Cothen, how your daughters
wrinkled their noses and puffed their waxed apple
cheeks, and the sons attended to their nose hairs
as the little clutch of journeymen musicians
you kept fiddled and squeaked, drops
of sweat plopping from their upper lips
as they labored over music too difficult to play
but which still said, plainly, O dumplings!
O zits! *macht auf* with the periwigs,
into the woods, the sunned air, the freshets
of vertiginous water, when you die you are dead
for so long no niceties of taffeta or toupee,
no good regard of the godful will redeem your death,
don't let any masses mislead you to studied solemnity,
serious doesn't mean solemn, necessarily, (signed:)
Papa Bach, Papa Bach, Papa Bach.

Thanksgiving

On the tube, the old parade:
they've shoveled the shit off the streets
to make room for the starlets and
Conan the Barbarian with that tight helmet
to keep his skull screwed down and
His Eminence the Archbishop of N.Y.
waves as though to say "howdy, folks,
I hope you're not contemplating
an abortion" and the Arkansas Razorback
Marching Band plays some of Mozart's
greatest hits from *Amadeus* and the sun
blesses everything like a kid
watching tv with one eye
on his homework and

I see myself there in a brown snowsuit
with a zippered hood, waving
a diminutive flag above the crowd
and yelling to my father "higher!
hold me higher!" in front on an automat
where I learned later bums & kids went
for free lemonade, got lemon wedges
from the condiment trays and sugar
to mix with free ice at the water cooler—
one of the few mercies the city provided
but stopped giving long since—and
to which my father took me for years
for his favorite restaurant meal,
automat beans, baked in little brown pots
with a thin glaze of pork grease on top
and explained, always, that there was no
other city in the world where you could put
quarters and nickels in a slot and
get a pot of beans like that and

here's a band from Williamsport, PA—
"a town that's more than just little League"
says Bobby Arnold the MC, who played
a corpse on *V*—doing its "unique" rendition
of "Stardust" beneath the world's first and largest
floating rubberized deconstructionist critic
masquerading as the Michelin Man and as far
as I can see this thing goes on forever,
dwarfs and Prince and minimum wage teens
carrying buckets and brooms behind
the Aleppo Shrine Horse Patrol and Placido Domingo
("hey man, don't step in the Placido Domingo!")

Changing the Name to Ochester

When other grandpas came to Ellis Island
the Immigration people asked "Name?"
and they said "Sergius Bronislaus Jgzywglywcz"
and the officer said, "ok, from now on your name's
Sarge Jerko," and Sarge trundled off to the Lower East Side
with a lead cross and a sausage wrapped in a hair shirt
and shared a tiny ill-lit room with eight *Landleute*
and next to a pot of boiling diapers began to carve
yo-yos to peddle on the street and forty years later
was Sarge Jerko, Inc., the Yo-Yo King,
but my grandfather was born in this country
(no one living knows anything about *his* parents)
and was an engineer for Con Edison
when he married the immigrant girl
Katherina Humrich who everybody said
was once very pretty but when I knew her
had a tight bun, thin German lips
and a nose which came to her chin;
her major pleasures were trips to Coney Island
with friends and frightening little children
by jumping out from behind curtains, after which
she cackled hilariously. This is all I know for certain
about my grandfather: 1) his name was Olshevski,
and he changed it shortly after his marriage,
when they were living in an Irish neighborhood,
2) while working at Con Ed he bought a yacht
my grandmother said, but my mother said, "Mom,
it was just a boat," 3) he left Katherina
after the fourth son was born, and she lived
in a tiny apartment on Chauncy Street
which smelled, even when I was eight,
like boiled diapers, 4) he was reported
to be handsome and have "a roving eye,"
5) my father and his brothers
all of whom are dead now
refused to go to his funeral
and never spoke of him.

This is a poem about forgiving Grandpa
for my not knowing him. And father, if you're
reading over my shoulder, I don't forget how
you had three cents spending money a week
and gave two cents to the church, or how
Uncle George, the baby who was everybody's
darling, couldn't go to college because he had
to work to support the family like everybody else
and how he became a fire chief in the City of New York,
and how Uncle Will, before he died of cancer,
became an advisor to La Guardia and made a bundle
by being appointed trustee of orphans' estates,
or how Uncle Frank, driving his battery truck
once was stopped by Will and La Gaurdia in their big car
and they chatted, and Uncle Frank—my favorite uncle,
neither Olshevski nor Ochester—still talks
about how his partner Paddy kept saying
"Bejasus, it was the Mayor,"
or how, because you had to support your brothers,
you couldn't marry till 30
and were engaged for eight years to my mother
who to this day loves you because you did
what you had to do, and how you built your business
going door-to-door selling insurance on Chauncy Street
and Myrtle Avenue till late at night, arguing and collecting
quarters and dimes from people who lived
in tiny apartments smelling of boiled diapers.
Nearly twenty years since your death, father,
and long ago I've forgiven you, and I think
you did love me really, and who am I, who was born
as you said, "with everything," to condemn
your bitterness toward your father who left you
with nothing?

I don't believe in original sin.
I believe if we're strong enough and gather our powers
we could work it out: no petty human misery,
no windrows of the dead slaughtered
in suicide charges, no hearts shrunken
and blackened like meat spitted
and held too long to the fire.
But what everybody knows
is enough to make you laugh
and to break your heart.
Grandpa, forty years after your death,
by the power vested in me as the oldest
living Ochester in the direct line I hereby
forgive you. And though you died,
my mother says, penniless and alone
with no one to talk to
I hope that when you abandoned your family
you lived well. I hope you sailed your 15-foot
yacht out into Long Island Sound
with a pretty woman on board and a bottle
of plum brandy. I hope that when the huge yacht
with "Jerko II" on the stern sailed by
you looked up and said "honey,
you'll be sailing one like that some day"
and that she giggled and said, "yeah,
hon, gimme a kiss" and afterward tilted
the bottle, and that the sun was shining
on the Sound, and that you enjoyed
the bitter smell of the brine and
the brilliance of the white scud and
that when you made love that night
it was good and lasted
a long, long time.

The Heart of Owl Country

Whatever blossoms is rooted
in the dark as, item,

the delicate purple comfrey flower
supported by a brutish taproot

that powers itself into the subsoil
and splits the shale a dozen feet

beneath me, so that the bumblebees
tumble in a drunken frenzy here, and

item, how if I tend my loneliness,
which is no rarer than yours,

friend, I grow stronger,
so that my fists open, and the garden

becomes a natural metaphor for what
we have always known:

that only by going deeply
as possible into our dark

can we discover ourselves
to others, and even though

the stutterer I have always been
would like to say, "we will never

die" I know that we will utterly
except for what we yield to friends

or progeny — that's the garden part —
and I remember now what I'd forgotten

for years, how, once, when we were
driving to my mother's, in New York State,

at twilight passing through a large marsh
my daughter said *look*! and in every dead

tree there was an owl, hundreds of them,
stupid in the light, like a faulty senate,

staring uncomprehendingly at the swamp
and the cars on the interstate, so still

one could have knocked them off their
perches with a stick and my daughter

screamed, delighted, "this must be
the heart of owl country!" and it

was: those soft fists of feathers
waiting for their hour, long

after we'd passed lifting into the spring air
on their solitary flights, each silent

in its large community, alert and perfect.

Kristine Dugas

It Is Too Cold to Change the Sheets

Hour after hour I lie listening
to my own movement;
a self-generated heat opening
to worlds without, your hands' touch
touching my touch. Severed,
the dull days die
without heat, and I most alive
in sleep, dreaming
anxiously, or, half-awake,
weighted by the covers like your love.

Indifferent is the world that keeps me from you.
Indifferently it cheats us from ourselves.
So, low beneath the sheets,
I slip out to you—
your heart, my heart, my body sinks,
weighted by the covers of the warm world
to you opening,
opening now.

Beverly Baranowski

The Power of Dreams

You probably don't know this
but while you sleep on an
airplane the stewardess watches
you. She sees how you curl
inward hugging yourself
how your head lolls back
the small drool starting.
She knows how you looked
as a child. The moment a seed
forms in the corner of your eye
she feels you dreaming in her body.
She bends over you for hours
checking your progress and
when you have it right
you all dream in unison
the aircraft hums along
at the proper pitch
she sits in her jumpseat
and closes her eyes.
Safe at last, held aloft
by the power of your dreams
you glide together toward
your separate and terrifying
destinations.

I Can Tell You

I can tell you about airplanes.
I've flown everywhere on airplanes and
I can tell you the best place to sit
on a 747 a DC10 a 727 or an Electra.
It all depends on if you smoke or
don't smoke, if you have kids or babies
if you have a broken arm or foot.
Sometimes you want to sit in the front row.
If you have kids you want that. A lot of tall
men like the front row because of leg room.
They forget about the crying babies.
Sometimes there's two or three and
one of them always creeps into the guy's lap,
bawling and drooling. The guy looks at you
and asks to be put in First Class, but you
always say "No." Don't ever sit in Row 51
on a 747. That's in the tail and it
whips back and forth like a crazy
boat trailer on windy days. You'll find six
bathrooms back there and the odor eats
you alive. You hold your breath the whole
time you're in one, pull your pants down
with one hand, hold the inside of your arm
over your face, breathe into your sleeve
for fresh air. I can tell you airplanes
make a lot of noise. Lots of odd sounds
you get used to and you can sense
if something's wrong. An exra ping
sets your heart pounding, your mind
spins over the steps of how to
open the door and inflate the chute.
You learn the way an aircraft leans
when it's happy, the pressure's just right
the air feels clean. You sing along
with it and sometimes the way

the pilots fly makes you feel
like floating in the middle of the aisle
with your coffee pot. Some days
the engines are uneasy all day,
can't seem to find the rhythm of flight,
passengers fidget, their heads
swivel around at every sound.
You're edgy and the pilot's crabby
and I can tell you, you'll be lucky
to walk away alive.

Bread

The staff of life is on diets now.
It's good for you, you need it.
Whole wheat's best, but I don't
like the looks of it. It has little
chunks of stuff in it. Trees.
Squirrel hairs. Coffee grounds.
Rambo eats whole wheat bread.
It makes your insides go all tan.
It causes strange yens for tofu
and herb tea. You begin to speak like
a lettuce head, broccoli is your brother.
Whole wheat bread disturbs your brain
makes you want to read philosophy
and discontinue shaving. You give up
sugar cookies and chocolate cake. You cry
in your sleep, the pillow soft as Wonder.
You forget about your lover,
everything soft in your life, you stay
alone to bake bread, you grind the grains
with your teeth so it's purely, wholey yours.
You grow skinny with anxiety about
your body, your blue veins change color,
your skin gets bumpy, you become roughage.
You go to the grocery store disguised
as a native, food gathering a tribal
activity, moving through the aisles
on hands and knees as down the rows
of living plants. You avoid the bread
aisle completely. You cannot tolerate
the laughter seeping through the cellophane.

Forgiveness

One day after my father died
my mother told me they'd known
a great deal of passion in their marriage.
I knew about their fights. The slammed
door freed him to go to the corner tavern
drink Boilermakers, play darts and pinball
tell jokes till closing. She continued
the fight without him, told him off good
as we sat silent and bug-eyed
on the green couch, though we knew
the finish. She always had the last word.
We turned on T.V., watched Ozzie & Harriet
bland as vanilla pudding till her
searing words eased out of the room.
She made popcorn and we leaned into her
licking our buttery hands till way past
our bedtime. Sometime during the night
the smell of whiskey and smoke held us
rubbed its beard against us, tucked us
in tight as we rolled like minnows
in his arms. It's good to know we were born
and lived through forgiveness and desire.
It's up to us to carry on the family
tradition. Keep the element of fire
in our eyes, make every day blaze alive.

Marilynne Thomas Walton

Farmer's Market

Outside, back of the mall
they cluster,
Sun blistered pick-up trucks —
Caves fortified with
tables of new potatoes,
skins furled, like radish roses.
Honey, jars of amber sun.
Leaf lettuce corsages; fingers of hairy carrots;
Zucchini trayed in neat rows, green
babies in a nursery.

The Hmong women hang their embroidery
like meadow flowers from an umbrella.
A woman in white shorts buys magenta and orange gladioli
too precious for money.
"Cut the snow peas like this," the Oriental man shows me.
Confused, I drop my parsley.
It is too much, too much to see, to
eat, to take back what the earth gave.

Linda Nemec Foster

History of the Toenails

A quiet, shy character (a male poet) in an American short story insists that toenails grow wild and uncontrollable in East Europe. There, they do not need conscious thought to thrive and flourish. They do it in spite of themselves, without thinking. He feels this part of the world is the only place where history really does matter and, in effect, allows the toenail to be nothing more, nothing less than a toenail. In Poland, Czechoslovakia, Hungary, and Romania old women sift through oppression in tight shoes, binding stockings and never bother to cut their toenails: they know it is the one part of themselves that is forever replenishing. A prime example — my grandmother from Krakow. Wild and uncontrollable at 86, she cursed her Cleveland-born sons and decided to live in the attic. Finally, she ran away from home in late January with no shoes, her bare feet clicking on the ice. The sound of hard, blue toenails long and curved over the edge of toes like naturally fitted tap shoes. The last image she left me with was of her dancing out a little secret code spelling VISTULA, ZAKOPANE, TATRA, JASNA GORA. Take off your shoes and learn it, she said.

Birthday Poem

For Anthony Jesse

I.
Our fathers' slow climb
up the stairs.
How the city was hot,
August, and hard to sleep:
men can't dream easy
in such heat;
only search a little
for their wives lying still,
lying closed then open.

And this hot night is for you
as well as for me.
The white cotton sheets stained —
our fathers' sweat, our mothers' skin.
We were born out of them
almost on the same day,
probably conceived the same night.

II.
1949 already owned our parents.
The post-war upward move:
suburbs and green shrubs,
plastic flamingoes on a neat lawn.
Their thin legs balancing the marriage
that lived in the house beyond —
completely brick, mortgaged.

Days of afternoon factory-shifts;
each wife understanding
nothing but this first pregnancy.
Her husband's body laid bare.
Each morning almost sinful
when she felt too sick
to get up and clean the house.

The nights forgave again and again:
a bird of blue glass, perched
in a white shadowbox,
would find the moonlight
and fly through dust.

III.
Twenty-two years for each of our lives.
This celebration has no candles
for lovers who almost share birthdays,
share dark nights in a rented room
where the only light comes from the stars:
stars that shape a goat, a virgin.

We shape the twins but not as brother/sister
and refuse to believe the predictions:
we will become dangerously similar; Gemini
in each of us will destroy the other.

But we cannot escape the one fate
that began with our parents'
slow movement in the same darkness,
which bore us, pushed us out,
into the air of a late May night.

Not our close births but our close lives
will prove the harder miracle.
Eye to open eye witnessing
how small we sometimes look,
how terribly lost and common.
And the love, just beginning.

Sharon Chmielarz

Reading Responsively

I sat in church. I heard.
First the preacher read from the pulpit.
Then the people from the pews.
Unbookish hands held blue hymnals
open; farmers read of light—"More
to be desired," they read, "than gold."
"Sweeter than the honey on the honeycomb."
I heard dark voices drone for light.
I heard little cries to abandon
all darkness in the heart
to the glimmer of light that shivers
under words in the Psalms.
But I was stubborn, I thought
what I had learned in my father's house
worked better. By Sunday dinner
one hour later, I was back
practicing the rule of darkness:
to save the sweetness of light
you reject it. The way I reject
my mother, to save her brightness
from the jealousy of my father.
In the afternoon when I go out
I wear a hat against light
that is hot and strong as irons.

From Jôsef in the Rest Home

I'm still alive.
My wife is dead.
She was smart—
a German.
She learnt how to sew.
I learnt how to save—
right from the start,
on the farm in Poland,
da! We were eighteen
eating out of one pot.

I learnt to eat fast.
I saved groszy, zloty
and bought my way out
of the First World War.
In the Second I saved
nylons and chocolate.
Cigarettes traded best
on the Black Market.

It'll happen again!
In America, the *Kommunisti*
will pound at the door
like in Riga. We were in bed.
We had to flee in the night
with our coats and children.
That Roosevelt, he sold us out!

My son looks down his nose
(German, like his mother's)
at the things I learnt.
Here in America he has everything
and never learnt about how you

hide bread and boiled eggs
for tomorrow; save cardboard
for floormats; aspirin,
big pins and bootstrings,
you can always use. In this room

I learnt if the draft
comes in the window
and the door is closed,
you get rheumatism.
But if the door is open
and the draft goes through
you get arthritis.

Someday my son
will learn this thing,
and he will remember
he laughed at his father.

Da! I learnt everything
I need to know, and more
just sitting here
by the t.v. tray.

First Snow

Mom sits by the living room window,
silent. She was waiting for snow
and got a visit from her daughter.
At first glance, they're the same
except when it comes, snow stays
longer, more like a friend.

Dad looks healthy in his chair,
rotund proof that God is male.
Mom looks old. She's given up
salvaging among the decisions
in God's cellar. She turns

from us both to watch
snow's coming—the suitor
who stands quietly outside,
inviting her out, bearing down
firmly on the door
without once using a fist.

Taking a Snow Bath

It's simple when there's powder snow.
You find a barren space—arched silence
between parents. You put on a cloak,
the color and sweep of bluejay wings
and then, so no one can see where it is
you're coming from, you sweep down—
cloak-tail, wing-sleeves gloriously
flying—Plunge! You're in diamond snow.
You come up in whatever character you want.
I choose Bird, bachelor aunt. She ruffles
her feathers, sputters at a bath
when the kitchen's cold. With a long
blue shiver, she works the snow down
through oil and dirt in her wings
taking every grain she needs to come clean,
then she flits her head and is gone . . .
The prints left behind are small
but the wingmarks, precise as knifecuts,
and the bad blood, pure.

Marriage of Two Old Men

Has he married my father? Have I married his?
What are two lonely old men doing in this house?
One from North Dakota, one from Poland.
They have no language in common!
Except a stubborn nature's — "*Stur!*"
Both refuse to tend the other's flock of geese
though they both want roast goose for supper.
What this marriage needs is a woman.
All the servant women in the house have died.
All the sluts have run away.
All the hardworkers have left for softer jobs.
And the sisters have married ambitious men.
These two left are too cheap to advertise for help.
What will happen to their house? the geese?
What will happen to us, Tad, without a woman?

Marie and Ella

Marie Coffin, my mother's neighbor on the south,
calls my mother, sick this fall, when geese flock
and fly in strings, tangling
and untangling over the two women's houses,
one widowed, one still living with the tyrant.
"Ella," the widow says, "go to the door and listen."
With the speed of 80-year-olds over rag rugs
they go to their doors and stand still while
the geese honk their way across heaven—
"We're leaving. We're leaving."
Marie and Ella don't applaud until the last wisp
of sound is gone. A sense is tendered—they've
been in concert, these geese and women,
who've seen the world, from both top and bottom.

Barry Silesky

Keeping Watch

a belated epithilamion for René and David

1
Between the old friends I hadn't
seen and the full moon
clearing the trees on the way
to its eclipse, the time never came
though I watched as the night went on,
the fire died to ember
and the party's laughter fell
to the neighbor's complaints.

Four of us drifted toward the beach
where two rangers said we couldn't
go: these are the rules. So we sat
by the side of the road and I looked
for a line or two: something about
a shadow nibbling away the moon,
this ambling toward morning; how night
crawls so long then suddenly it's over . . .

the way we talked about baseball,
rules, the fire of other campers;
then half the silver was gone,
the dark half so ordinary we kept
staring at the memory
of what was there: the fat shine
that crept away while half the country
slept. I wanted to explain how it

fit with a man and a woman
on the way to the beach
where they'll meet again,
this time for good, amid friends,
the sun, all the broken hours
they've come through. What do we say
as they turn to face the light,
the darkened moon left behind?

2
Alone in this bar looking out
at the rain, an old friend stops

on her way up the street; she's been
wandering through the past: her father's

whiskey, the failure of words, the work
she still doesn't know how to

finish. Years ago we might have talked
for hours, drunk into the dark,

eyes lighting a way through the night
we couldn't let go. We'd call the moon

a fine excuse, no one married,
and breakfast whatever we wanted.

But the skin gets so sticky it's dangerous
to answer the phone, and we sail

the edge of our circular nights
begging the room to stop.

Now you tell me you're late
to meet your husband, and we've learned

what's broken won't be fixed
by our words. He's waiting

for steps to sound in the hall,
the key to turn in the lock.

In another dark corner, a man
is laughing. He brushes a strand

of hair from the face of the woman
beside him. She leans to touch

his arm. We know what this means.
So you leave, only a little late,

and send your best to my wife.
We've learned it is enough.

3
Tonight the moon's still full behind the storm,
the shadow's passed and you're married.
The rules say this is just the beginning.
I could have talked about birds, those clichés
of equivocal song, or the clearing
I stumbled on somewhere in the woods;
but it's a year since my own wedding,
and again we're in a bar as if to see
what's changed. You say it's about mountains,
the rise and fall of these days, and we talk
about the weather in the kitchen, the stranger
we can't ignore calling from the corner,
and defending our side of the room whatever
sleazy motel we've given up for homemade
soup and a cat. Now you're supposed to
put on weight, build a closet; and my job
is the landlord, a broken chair, Cleveland
every other Thanksgiving. Listen:
there's always a voice pulling us
in, a hand brushing a hand, and it comes
down to choices: a thousand bars in this city
and one of them always open, but now we drain
the last glass and stumble into the street, finally
headed for home. It's about time.

Working on the Roof

The thing is to pay attention.
You've heard it so often already
you're half asleep, but the rafters
are narrow, the pitch just steep enough
that the least lapse will send you back
over the edge and you'll never be here
again. You can do it for years—
the sheer charge of that thin margin
the wave you live to crest on;
and you love to make it look easy,
though that requires an audience;
alone the stakes are different.
Because it never lasts, of course—
the roof goes on, you blink,
another house is finished. You lean out
to fasten the final piece of soffit,
or climb the hundredth time
to trim some last edge clean,
already watching for the next swell
or clinging to the last, and suddenly
you've forgotten where you are:
that's when the ladder slips,
the whole thing collapses
and you're on your back in the fog.
Somewhere the house goes on, but now
the tools keep drifting by, each one
a choice you're helpless to reach,
mocking your outstretched arms.
The thing is to pay attention.
Because you're always alone in the end,
walking that too thin plank out into the space
where only the air can bear you.

A Day in the Country

1

The attraction's undeniable. The haystacks lined up
like seasons, each pair a tribute to what goes on,
an age of plenty—food, time, space, and today
when the room's not crowded, it almost seems true.
Except for the muddy drone of the guidephones,
the overperfumed matron who shoulders in the way, the weather
doesn't exist. The sky's red blushes in the field, seeps into
the grain, and there's no one else in the frame.
It's a way of being alone, and warm, the broken
light spreading from one view to the next, folding us
into this day we came to believe. An odd sensation—
those fields so clear in the distance, the stacks so sure,
and yet the closer the eyes get, the more they come
apart, dissolving into the light the paint tries to contain.

2

Just south of the hospital next to the projects,
the piles of litter on lawns, the battered cars,
the school doors are chained, and I was lucky
to find someone to show me the one open
to the basement, and a way through
the pipes and boilers to the halls.
I remember the year I worked in a junior high
that could have been this: the girl who ran off
with my books when I took her cigarettes, dope
in the john, booze in purses, the gun
the teacher next door talked a student out of . . .
Now they show me how they can't spell their street,
their name, and the girl who's pregnant with her
third: ". . . got to unnerstand this is the get-toe,"
the teacher's spondee brittle as glass. I tell them
something about metaphor; the resemblance of disparate

shapes I've seen students find; a way to enter
a picture, to find something they've never
seen; and on the way out, for just an instant, I imagine
my tire's flat and the thugs in the shadows appear
to beat me out of everything they think I've got.

3

Most I remember the lone figure
on a hill above the village. Folded in a coat,
hands empty, he's making his way
through stunted trees; or he's stopped
to look at what's ahead. Either way, we only see
his back, a blur like the rest of the scene.
And it's winter; the snow keeps drawing me
in — I can almost forget where I am. So time spreads
space the way painters spread light until we get lost
in those surfaces; we have to back away to be sure
what's gone on. But after an hour or two,
we're listening again for the phone, missing
the traffic. It's a beautiful country,
and impossible. Broken glass carpets the lot outside,
and it's not enough that the tire's not flat.
"A boy is a forest," the metaphor went. If he's lucky
there's a trail. If he's lucky, he finds it,
and he's home before dark. We've got to
find the right distance to see.

The New Tenants

The coffee cup's broken handle lies
in the glint of paper clips, the glass
I shattered this morning, and all
the things that left me. They're flying
into October, its red painting the way

to the future we love to believe in,
and slowly we begin again to imagine
those gorgeous clothes, the possibilities
of afternoon dressing the wide meadow,
each delicate thread completing our hands.

Too bad the needle is always buried
in the drawer we hate to open.
Tomorrow we swear we'll rearrange
that rummage, but the objects keep putting on
weight, winding into each other

like those smugly content couples
no one really knows, while the years
draw their circles around the house
we always wanted to live in, a prospect
more frightening than anyone admits.

These imagined glimpses add up
to the faded paint, the shrieking
pump that does what we ask,
but so painfully all the guests remark.

Alone, we can forget
the complaints, the unmowed yard,
the brightness of other houses
with their perfect gardens
and chickens that always lay.
Is this what they mean by older?

How a conversation about flight turns
into the objects it couldn't contain
still where they've always been—
a postcard taped to the wall, dust
frosting the piano . . .? If only,

I begin again, but still don't know
enough to carry it off,
and then the afternoon is over,
its oily residue filming the glass,
but so faintly I barely notice

the sagging wires the pigeons have left
like leftover promises scattered
through the city; the way I felt
about that house in the middle
of making it; the new tenants taking over.

Anna Wasescha

The Storm

T he woman walked around the room like a cat and then turned toward the window as though someone had just told her a tornado was coming up. Do you understand why I called you? the man was saying, I lost control of my car, my wife left me a note saying thanks for your time, I didn't know who else to call, I figured you'd understand. He wouldn't stop saying that, she knew that he wouldn't stop. Outside the snow lay flat and quiet. It reminded her of the farm up north and of the moon. She had things on her mind. When the baby had started forming inside her she knew it looked like him. It was darker and hairier and it had bad eyes. That it had been conceived in September was nice. Summer is nice. . .and hot, like bricks on a river levee. Hot and damp and kind of red around the edges. She wondered if it had been a boy. Any baby she would ever have would look like the father. She knew that too. When she was hit from the rear after the abortion her car had looked like the other car. It made sense. And he ran. That too made sense. In the morning she had showered and put on her clothes and run out the door without thinking. Now it was important to think, but it was the same. Someone was chasing her. Someone was coming across a frozen field from the west with the sun hanging just to the left of his shoulder. All the frozen fields in Kansas can't stop the river, or the men, in great herds like buffalo and owls coming down cold and hard around her asking her to dance, on the river. It isn't easy. Now was the time to turn and try to think, try to say things that make sense. She could still hear him. I know what's bothering you, I know the root of your problem. You thought up all those things we could do this summer, and you got into it, and your eyes flashed like fire in the night and your feet came off the ground like great seabirds over the water and you wanted it hard and you knew it would never happen. She looked from the window to his dark face and then back again. When they had surrounded her in the hospital and held her down and put the needle in her arm she had thought of him holding her. When she had put her feet in the stirrups and spread her knees she tried to picture his face when he kissed her, tried to remember what clothes he was wearing the last time she saw him. It hadn't worked. He had come up to her and stood with the broken shafts of corn at his feet and the sun resting on the horizon and had begun to disappear, one piece at a time, with every gesture and word he gave her. She wasn't dancing. Well I'm not angry he was saying. I'm actually feeling pretty happy today, you know how my moods are. I'm not mad at you you know. The woman placed the tips of her fingers across the flat surface of the window sill and lay her head down on them. She was tired, and on that field where she stood watching, always, for her men, the last pitch of the sun faded away from her feet toward the mountains out further west than she might ever travel, her standing there as though on a verandah, her hands in her apron pockets, leaning back on her heels. She was waiting for the storm.

Victor Contoski

A Tour of the State Capitol: Topeka

Ad astra per aspera
"to the stars through difficulty"

the sandstone foundation
    laid in the fall of 1866
    crumbled in the spring of 1867

    replaced by limestone
    per aspera
    and the building grew.

Under the stone of the east wing
a spring
in the Great American Desert
    a sign to God's people.

Marble from overseas
    blue-gray Belgian marble
    onyx from Mexico
    Italian Carrara

laid layer by layer
on the backs
    of the working men
    and working women of Kansas

Honduras mahogany for the president's rostrum
in the Senate Chamber

twenty-eight copper columns
    with hand-hammered morning glories and roses
    watered by the hidden spring
        the miracle of taxes.

The west wind followed

wainscoting trimmed with Italian Carrara
Brocelian marble panels
Belgian black marble
    at the foot of the columns
jasper in the east wall.

Between the two wings
rose the great stone bird of the dome
304 feet into the air
    ad astra
the cupola stretching
    higher and higher
    like the ambition of Ozymandias
    like the hopes of the people of Kansas.

Lewis and Clark and Coronado
    look up from the first floor.
The scouts and Indians at the Battle of Arikaree
    stop fighting and look up.
The sod-busters and railroad workers
and people in the wagon trains
and the people in the old fashioned cage elevator
and the old fashioned cage elevator itself
    stop and look up.

On the second floor
the portrait of Dwight D. Eisenhower
and the portrait of Charles Curtis
    look up.

In the office of the Secretary of State
the modified octagonal table
built by a prisoner in Lansing
with over 2,000 pieces of wood
around the great U.S. seal in the center
    looks up.

Colonel John C. Freemont
the threshers and well diggers
the school teachers and the traveler
 leaning into the blizzard
 as he makes for the Governor's Mansion
 at Lecompton *per aspera*
  look up.

The statues of Dwight D. Eisenhower of Abilene
 William Allen White of Emporia
 Arthur Capper of Topeka
 and Amelia Earhart of Atchison
 strain
  to turn their stone necks
  toward the dome.

The Kansas Senate in the East Wing
and the Kansas House in the West Wing
 pause at their grand desks
 pause in the marble corridors
  and look up.

The legislative staffs
 polishing the shoes of their masters
 polishing the black and white Georgian marble
 on the wainscoting of the fourth floor
  look up.

The committee rooms and legislative offices
on the top floor fall silent
and look up at the stairway into the dome
and into the dome itself *ad astra*

the great heavenly dome
 sky blue
 eight flags like birds fluttering
  red blue yellow white flashing
  against the dark center of the circle
   the wind-rose.

Nobody moves.
Nobody breathes

as the legislators and committees
and taxpayers taking the tour
and statues and paintings
and offices and elevators
and Carrara marble and Honduras mahogany
all look up into the dome
    like worshippers.

At the very top
    jutting into the sky
        the still point
        the center

a twitch
    something
another twitch
    in slow motion something is falling
    slowly falling

a wrench
    falling
        from the dome of the capitol
    tumbling
        as if in slow motion
            down down

                through space
                through time
                    head over handle
                    handle over head

and after it
a man

.

John Cave
    iron worker
    24 years old in 1890

falling as in a dream
tumbling
    in slow motion
        from past to present to future

        head over heels
        heels over head

from the dome to the fourth floor
    hitting the polished marble
    like a sack of wheat
        and bouncing
            from floor to floor
            with a dull sound
                like a taxpayer groaning.

The windows in the East Wing
turn into little soundless o's.

Dwight D. Eisenhower
    folds his arms.
William Allen White
    puts his left hand in his pocket.
Arthur Capper clutches his hat
    and stares straight ahead.
Amelia Earhart
    remembers the wind in her face

as John Cave falls
    from floor to floor to floor
    of the state capitol
        head over heels
        heels over head.

His body—*thud*! bounces
    one last time
        twitches
            and stops

but his brains go on
    through his skullcase
        all the way down to the basement

where they lie
    with the hopes of the Kansas taxpayers
    and the dreams of Ozymandias
    and the original sandstone foundation of 1866
        that has crumbled *per aspera*
            to a mass of mud.

A Dream of Old Classmates

The Alexander Ramsey House, St. Paul

August again 1961
early evening
under the elm trees

all my old classmates
sit on the floor of an old house
huge as the elms.

Doc Whiting smiles
as he calls role
through his gray mustache
his bald head shining
like a streetlight:
       Dan Cashman . . .
       Betsy Edelson . . .
       Morris Edelson . . .
       Richard Halverson . . .
       Ed Ochester . . .
       Hugh Olmsted . . .
       Hertha Schulze . . .

The lights of the parlor
shine down
on their unmarked faces

as they sit on the polished wood floor
discussing the lesson for the day
       gesturing
       laughing softly
       talking in a steady hum.

Suddenly the big front door
swings silently open

as if on cue
the class gets up and goes out.

Oh no, says Doc, shaking his head
Now they'll never come back.

I run out.
Wait! Come back. It isn't finished.

But already they are wandering off
in twos and threes
under the leaves and branches
of the huge elms
into the darkness

and only the crickets speak
under the streetlights

as I hurry back to the big house
of Alexander Ramsey
which is now dark and silent.

Bridge

for my uncle, Francis Helgesen

The living
study their hands.

Someone bends over slowly
his cards flutter down
and he falls.

Uncle father husband
he does not move.

One calls the ambulance.
Others pick him up carefully
carefully lay him on the couch.

Doctors appear
shaking their heads.

Life systems go on
and then go off.

What remains
goes to science.

Then one by one
we pick up memories
scattered like cards

aces and kings

shuffle them

cut
and deal.

Municipal Auditorium: Kansas City

Limestone
concrete and steel
a bunker of the arts

Municipal Auditorium squats
in helmet and shoulderpads.

Inside
awaiting the snap:
    exhibitions
    actors
    ushers in bright red uniforms
    programs stacked by the aisles
    instruments finding their pitch
    jugglers rehearsing

    Virgil Thompson
    Hans Swieger

    circuses and magicians

    protected from traffic and weather
    by an overweight giant
    that remembers school pageants
    cotton candy and clowns
    and "Country Gardens" on the piano.

Capitol Hill: Omaha Central High School

High on Capitol Hill
this Nebraska parthenon

Corinthian pillars
stand out in the morning sun
like five good students
raising their hands.

Windows and pilasters
parade proudly
before downtown Omaha—
Art, Music, Science, and Drama
marching up for their degrees

where once the territorial legislature
convened with bludgeons
brickbats and pistols
to discuss the location
of the state capitol.

The school day ends.
Children disperse.

And in the silence of evening
Capitol Hill looks southwestward
toward Lincoln

like a proud old woman
who had a fine beau
when she was young
and lost him.

Helen Degen Cohen

Hawaii, AH

I am the mistress of a conservative. The other characters are an activist, an artist, a girl on rollerskates, and—the conservative himself, whom I've almost forgotten. At any rate, there we were, and it may have been this business of having for a setting a place like Hawaii.

Hawaii. Where so little happens, the people themselves become more visible. Normally the smaller the town, the more recognized, though less pronounced, they are. They see each other in relation to family, the haves or have nots, the brains or idiots. But Hawaii has its own peculiarities, totally hidden from the tourist who unwittingly supports them. For one thing, it has a class system. Yes. For another, there is a scarcity of causes; thus the causes at hand, like the people, are both indulged and ignored, drowned in food, sunshine, job-hunting, clothes.

There is a bright, fresh-flower studded little cemetery in Hilo that looks like a box of cream and coral candy, because of the spread of many bouquets, partially shaded with Japanese umbrella-like trees. One can see the clusters of creamy coral, gold, and white flowers, as one drives by. It is somewhat surreal. And even in the tourist section the dense, luxurious street of banyon trees, perpetually shaded and dark, has about it an air of transience, with its immemorial Names of the Famous labelling each tree at its foot on nostalgic plaques—a bit surreal, as if even this street of shaded hotels were in a way a mausoleum one is only passing through, the rainbows on the ocean side of the hotels meant only for the haze in one's eyes, not even for the cameras. Women of all sizes walk in and out of restaurants and cars in ground-length floral dresses which ought to be, but aren't, ceremonial. Nothing is very ceremonial. When the volcano went off at 8 p.m. there were only a handful of people watching it from the side of the road, with only a few police cars parked alongside. In a painting on a wall of the volcano museum restaurant, Peles, Goddess of Fire, her wild hair menacing, tries to impact on the flow of visitors, eaters mainly. Everything passes, flows out from between the fingers cooler than lava, like cool surfers between the waves. It is hard to hold onto anything.

There they are, I among them, guests here, visitors from the mainland, at the activist's house for the day. The conservative introduces the mistress to the activist, who is watching television. The window of his ranch-house living room overlooks an exotic to mainlanders front yard of coconut and guava and other thick-leaved trees, a front yard which leads onto a strangely suburban street straight out of the midwest: clean split-levels, here and there a tree—though behind the street and close below it is the live ocean. An immaculate open suburban block, good enough for doctors. The mistress has been looking out the window for signs of the ocean, reassurance. When in comes the activist's sister, the artist.

She has come to cook dinner for some reason. She walks from room to room, making beds, talking idly about her brother's activities. It seems that he helps a "peace farm" somewhere, by buying their jellies and selling them in town. He has done some painting for them as well. The mistress is most attentive, but the artist, having said this much and lifted up a rug, disappears suddenly. Then returns, as abruptly, to take the mistress for a walk, and two daughters come along from somewhere, one on either side, chatting idly. The mistress enjoys their company, not knowing that soon they will vanish once more. As they walk the artist plucks several Hawaiian flowers that grow as weeds along the street, for the mistress to admire. In fact, she puts one in her hair. They also find a fallen coconut, as if it were an ordinary acorn.

Back in the house the Thursday night favorites are on and the activist's friends are busy watching, with a beer and an occasional comment. On looking closer, one may even notice the conservative, muted in a shadow, also watching. He looks up, greeting his mistress back from her walk, obviously pleased to see her; but immediately the artist invites her into the kitchen to help cook or something. The conservative appears a bit lost or lonely. The activist is nodding and smiling passively, as his friend from Texas talks about politics, schools, religion, crime, and the conservative dozes on and off in his corner. In the kitchen the mistress drools over plates of vegatarian chop suey and salads, marvels at the coconut being split open, listens to white Hawaiian (Kamaaina) concerns. Education is terrible in Hawaii, especially for the white minority, for whom there simply aren't any good enough schools. Why is that? Because of the illiteracy among the natives, the low standards; there is prejudice against the whites, who have difficult times finding jobs. When jobs do come up, the whites are the last to get them.

Is that right.

Yes, the artist's four children are constantly trying to find work and she herself is between jobs. She's staying here with her brother temporarily. She is very attractive, very friendly and open, with direct, trusting eyes. The mistress cuts through the midwestern kitchen to the palms in the living room window. She feels like a guest here, as everywhere, a strong, unsettling feeling which makes her a bit proud. A peace farm.

The talk over the buffet style dinner-in-the-lap is mainly between the mistress and the activist's avidly conversant friend from Texas, about causes, crime and education, school and gangs. The mistress feels herself becoming involved and lowers her voice. The activist has promised her (and the conservative) to take them out to the peace farm, where he and several others—students?—work at the double task of trying to keep Hawaii nuclear free and living off the land. Tomorrow, possibly.

Tomorrow, and the scene shifts slightly. Once more the conservative and the mistress arrive at the activist's house. They stand outside it, between the track house on the right and the sea below on the left, waiting. There is no artist on the scene this time, but a girl about eighteen comes out of the house on rollerskates, followed by the activist, a boyish-looking man of about 50, trim and suntanned, who makes the conservative look old and pallid and the mistress fat and aging. The tall, svelte girl with obvious breasts like baseballs, her blonde hair pulled back in a bushy pony tail, rides slow circles around the car, rides in and out of the house; pulls a camera out of her jeans pocket as she rides, and places a change-purse in the pocket. She fits herself into the passenger seat, the activist looking at her appreciatively from his driver's seat, the conservative and mistress watching from behind, the conservative's eyes hazy.

In the car the mistress is brimming with questions, as she looks out the windows at Hawaiian sidewalks, Hawaiian street names on the street signs passing by, noticing how few letters are used in the spelling, how often they repeat. Twelve letters. K's and L's and H's and W's and softly repeating rhyming vowels. Soft, a sad, repetitive sound, like the waves. Easy for the natives to learn, she is told. It *has* to be easy. They only use 12? — they think — letters in the alphabet. The mistress tries to picture the natives' thought processes undulating soft and uncomplicated, but the faces that pass on the sidewalk, in the busses, are rugged, practical, and private. Not only non-white, but a mixture of sea and sun and a warring history. A whaling, warring, boat-racing history for the males, not entirely oriental, not entirely anything. The mistress can't find any typical Hawaiians, any typical Hawaiian music. Often she has looked around her. She listens for the smooth songs one associates with Hawaii, but there aren't any. There is no music. The people are making a living. Riding busses. Using a short-cut language, going to bad schools and taking jobs from the whites? The mistress won't get to talk to a native, only kamaainas. These people in their kitchens and living rooms. But at least she'll see a peace farm. Never mind the sunsets or the golden beaches. A peace farm. The conservative, watching her, is proud to have come up with the activist. He knew she would appreciate this. He closes his eyes as the car passes small houses and short green trees. Then stops abruptly.

The girl on roller skates rolls towering out of the car, across some gravel, and into a little store on the highway. She comes back with a bagful of something and fits herself back into the front seat. Turns around and offers the white bag to the mistress — ah, sprouts — who is pleasantly reminded of the 60's, the spirit of sharing, growing your own food. Sprouts. The conservative smiles, declines at first, then tries a few. The activist is talking about the terrain, pointing to the plants, sugar cane, a mellow look on his face. (Has he ever been to jail, the mistress will ask of the conservative.) He sells real estate part-time, fairly successfully, and augments his lifestyle with some money from a former life on the mainland, before he chucked it all. He drives onto a dirt road, the mistress listening with appreciation.

They drive through lumpy farm country, fields planted with unusual green, stocky trees like those in children's picture books, lavish, close-to-the-ground trees. Ipa, used for humus, for food, for frying as cottage-fried potatoes. Guava trees with green guavas on them. Muddy plots planted like victory gardens, mud between boards, ahead an open half-finished structure of wood, then a table out in the open shade — an oriental man cooking something on a little stove. Everything outside. It reminds her of camp. Oh, the mistress exclaims, at last she can exclaim about something. They are all introduced to the "community" of 3 who hold down the peace farm: the activist's friend, a super-activist; and a tall, solid woman. The old oriental cook frying ipu in the open air looks up from some distance away. It smells good. On several tables among trees, as if at a rummage sale, are household items waiting for the house to be completed, for corners and cupboards. The party is taken onto the wooden floor of the future house, from future room to future room, introduced to the work that still needs to be done.

Perhaps she can tell the midwest about it. Has the midwest been told about this, exclaims the mistress. The super-activist looks interested, encouraged, lights a cigarette, looks up quickly and then down at the ground. Surely one can read about this *somewhere*, says the mistress, meaning outside of Hawaii of course. Is the mistress a reporter? No, she chuckles, but couldn't she tell this to a couple of reporters back home? They look at her, hopefully? It spurs some action. The solid woman, wearing mud-proof boots, takes them (the conservative too) on a tour, between the as-yet ceilingless walls, out between tropical trees, to the outhouse. Like a tree-house, exclaims the mistress. Back at the *house*, on tables against two completed walls, the mistress notices the cluster of jams in jars, and offers to buy one. The super-activist is seriously grateful. It'll pay for bread and milk for a week.

The conservative is grateful to the activist, the mistress proud of the conservative. Who would have thought that he would know such people. That Hawaii would be — earthy. And rugged. And —

everything. She looks around her, at the varied terrain. The Big Island is as varied as—a continent. She'd expected the land to be mock-velvet, the language trite, the streets walled off with white hotels, Don Ho crooning out of nightclub windows, grass skirts smothering the drugstores. The conservative is proud, and a little tired. He looks at his watch. The mistress sees him and he yawns, scratches his side, and smiles. The girl on roller-skates offers to take their picture, as they walk around the future living room, and they pose behind jars of jelly, the strange smells of new wood and surrounding mud and vegetation in their nostrils.

The activist has all this time been nearly ignored, his role of educating his guests taken over by the super-activist and the powerful outdoor woman, who gives the facts, on being questioned, about committee work, the fight against the military, peace. The mistress sucks her breath in at the way the super-activist keeps his eyes down—to keep the sparks from flying out, she thinks. He could set the place on fire. The activist looks on, from the side, the conservative smiles, asks a few practical questions. How is the house built? How is the place financed?

He's not the least bit afraid, thinks the mistress. Yet there are jails, policemen, pockets of fire. Volcanoes. The only erupting volcano in the world is here. They will see it tonight. The conservative yawns, his question answered.

From the table, a little distance away, the old oriental looks up and past them, through them, as if seeing nothing, as he eats his fried dinner, his flat face a gray moon, one of a million shapes of the night to come. A common enough oriental visage on the islands yet alone here on the peace farm, he is a man aside, not really among the solitary group of whites.

The mistress puts her hand through the conservative's elbow, and he gives her an approving look, fatherly and faithful, as he might in an old church where the stone saints need protecting from time and the weather and yet must be worshipped all the same, since there is that something in them, be it born of man or God, that can't be denied, something like the woman beside him, which must be paid for, by those who can afford it, of course. He expands his shoulders a little.

The girl on rollerskates stumbles from board to mud, then across to the car, and disappears into it. The activist follows her and they wait there. The super-activist keeps talking, digging his words like stakes into the ground, only half-aware of his audience. His eyes dart occasionally as if at some hostile destiny, thumb and forefinger pinching the cigarette, his teeshirt so worn, so ancient it commands respect. When he finally looks up it's as if he has no body, no voice, only a remote pit burning deep behind the sockets of his eyes, so deep that even he can't reach it, and he squints a little.

They have some fried "potatoes," they walk around the limited grounds.

The superactivist keeps on talking, in his clipped way, but the audience begins to tire. Or is it the mistress. The conservative has waited for this moment. He suggests that they leave. The man and woman follow them to the car, whose darkness has long since enveloped the activist and the girl on rollerskates.

We have left all that behind us, a day in the life of a peace farm. The danger in the man's eyes. We drive on.

Slowly the day fades, tangentially, somehow reminiscent of tourists as they pass between leis of hishi and coral, tee-shirts and canvas travel bags, blood-red sunsets and fire-blue shirts, tired from the long day's sights and restaurants, thinning out along with the daylight. The goods in the open-air shops take on new phosphorescence. Their glow-in-the-dark spreads out, intensifies, in open doorways, in shop windows; the characters thin out, a gradual silence washes over them, a second silence coming in, like the powerful surfers, on the waves. We are once more alone with each other. And later, alone. The beads and hats and surfboards glow with a power that outshines the night and its mysteries, in whose shadows the frothing mountain hides. When I think of Hawaii, I remember that I am the mistress of a conservative. I remember who I am.

Nicole Niemi

Our Florida Vacation

Noon.
The asphalt is lava.
We lie around on single beds with blue light TV tans.
The curtains pulled, we are watching a game show.
Bob Barker is beautiful and frightening:
he is our prophet.
The room is as cold as a dream.
The motor court is as lovely as it should be.
There is a housewife who wants door number 3.
We are feeling gracious as she wins a fur coat,
it is something we do not need.
We flash our smiles, our pina colada smiles,
she cannot see us.
The ice machine spits forth water diamonds.
We can have it all, it's all behind the curtain.

John Minczeski

Spring Comes to Lanesboro

The hardwoods fade into night,
branches stippled with brown and green fur
silent as three deer shying home
into the brush off the highway.

The thinnest of moons nudges Venus
over a bluff of the Root River Valley.
The way the road curves to follow the river,
the moon spirals as it declines.

Rattlers sleep in the sandstone caves
schoolboys scratch their names in—
things that disappear and come back
for us who keep the faith

and even for those that don't
like the couple loading
what's left of their antique store
into a pickup and an old Mercedes

and up highway 8 to Rochester
or the cities. Among the various languages
of this world, an old man sits at a table
tearing his bread. A voice like a creek

rumbling down to the river, the river
to a bigger river . . .
In the narrow valley between these bluffs,
oaks fountain up into faint-green stars

above the hydro-electric plant.
I hear the man's voice over and over—
the earth itself is good the way it is,
just stay here. The rest is easy.

Columbines / Summer / 1982

Columbines are blooming right now, between the honeysuckle
and bleeding heart. They are tucked out of sight, quietly,
like their cousins in Jelenie Gora. They could be pedestrians
walking down a sidewalk past a plainclothes man
while giving no sign of passing information.

They are so barely blue they could be used for paper
or prototypes of a future that shoots ahead at full speed,
darts backward at the same time and manages
with difficulty, to stay in one place. Grackles,
in washboard voices no one understands, give orders
from the ridge of the garage I'll tear down soon.
I'm already nostalgic for its swayback roof
and useless sentry boxes beside the broken door.

There are no chickens here and the sky is clouding over.
This is not a country where flowers get handed down
generation after generation, I don't know Polish,
and I'm losing an argument among these red flowers that will
never resemble blood, and blue ones so pale
they have given up claims to royalty forever.

Asphalt

At St. Stans, back in seventh grade,
a Black girl was sweet on my friend, Dave.
She didn't go to our school, just passed
through the playground on her way from lunch
with two friends shy at being
in this suddenly White world.
Dave hid behind a clump of us boys
trying to act as if chain reactions
weren't happening as we bumped into each other
and desperately looked for some horizon
to gaze beyond. Sometimes she found him
and had him walk with her on the other side
of the brick church,
her two friends hurrying ahead,
and then an extra block, alone.
We teased Dave for kissing her.
Mostly he just hid when she called.
Sometimes she'd take a swipe at him
with her pocketbook. Once she sang out to us,
"Oh boys, have you seen Dave?" when I,
maybe out of jealousy
at what could have passed for love,
pointed him out in the alcove that led
to the boiler room and Roman-the-Janitor's shop.
He came out, she put her arm through his,
and looked at him with kindness.
Part of me is always back there in that spring,
Diane and Dave walking away from us.
When he comes back to the playground,
he shoves me into the wall
and tells me never to do it again.
Part of me smiled, and part of me was sweaty
with seventh grade. Eighth grade,
she didn't come around any more.

I supposed white boys weren't worth the trouble.
A rumor goes she had a kid to get even with a system
that had no place for her. I think, if anything,
it would have been a son. Twenty-six years later
he leans against a white Chevy near Chapin Street
and Western and watches kids shoot baskets
behind Kaley school. The ball thunks steady
on the asphalt, slaps the backstop and through
the hoop with a metallic rattle.
The pole it's all attached to seems as straight
as any tree that springs out of the very
center of the earth.

My Name

for Victor Contoski

My name arrived from Poland in 1910 stowed away
in the engine room of a Swiss freighter. The cook took
pity on it and every day brought sausages, berries and
milk. My name for two weeks was deafened by the sound
of pistons and the turning of the twin screws.
My name, without a passport or an extra change of clothes.
Without a tooth brush or brown shopping bag,
swam to Staten Island, barely missed being eaten by sharks.
My name didn't know English. It was taken
in by potato farmers and learned to drive trucks
and drink beer. My name tripped
over a cabbage and was cut in half by a harrow.
Thus I was born. I have given it years of pain.
My name has forgotten how to cry.

Wild Rose

After Sonny Rollins for Seraphim Minczewski

I can almost hear the words
in the snow and weeping that comes
from a warm place though I've long
given up saying where that is
and in something as cold
as Minnesota tonight
there is a door
in this music that lets in no drafts,
that says there are 99 steps
on the stairway to heaven
and 99 years to climb them,
inhaling the smoke of our ancestors
the fields of Seraphim,
a wild rose like dusk
that indirect color after love
among the sun's dynasties,
another thing born without wings.

Contributor Notes

John Minczeski is the author of two poetry collections, *The Spiders* and *The Reconstruction of Light* both from New Rivers. He is the recipient of fellowships from the National Endowment for the Arts and The Bush Foundation. His work has appeared in *ACM*, *Abraxas*, *Kansas Quarterly*, and other journals. He lives in St. Paul where he teaches with the Writers-in-the-Schools program.

Paul Petroff (Piotrkowski) was born in Kielce, Poland. At the age of thirteen, he emigrated to Canada with his mother. In 1938 he moved to New York. During World War II he was involved with an intelligence unit, edited photographs, worked as a mapmaker for General Patton and also designed propaganda leaflets that were dropped behind German lines. For his efforts, he was awarded the Legion of Merit. After the war he made experimental films and worked as set designer for films. It was as a set designer that he developed an expertise with optics and lighting and became serious about still photography. He has traveled and photographed in Peru and Mexico and India. His most recent show was at the Bryant Library Gallery in New York last December where he was also commissioned to do a sculpture based on the Statue of Liberty.

Keith Abbott was born in Tacoma, Washington and grew up in the Northwest. He is the author of three novels and has been published in German, Italian and Russian anthologies. A collection of his short stories from the Northwest, *First Thing Coming*, has just been released by Coffeehouse Press.

Beverly Baranowski has published poems in *Milkweed Chronicle*, *The Lake Street Review* and other publications. She is also a visual artist, a new mother, and lives in Minneapolis.

Marek Baterowicz was born in Cracow in 1944. He has a doctorate in Romance languages and has translated extensively from contemporary French and Spanish poetry. He was an active member of Solidarity and now lives in exile — most recently in Madrid. His latest book of poetry is *Lamiac Galezie Ciszy* (*Breaking the Branches of Silence*), 1980.

Magda Bogin's great-grandmother Julia was born in the Carpathian village of Tlumacz, no longer in Poland. Other towns mentioned in family records have also slipped their moorings. Most of Julia's family was wiped out during WWII. Bogin's translations from the Spanish include *Here's Looking At You, Jesus* by Elena Poniatowska (Pantheon, 1987) and *House of the Spirits* by Isabel Allende (Knopf, 1985). A novel, *Natalya, God's Messenger* will be published by Harper & Row next year.

Anthony Bukoski's first collection of stories, *Twelve Below Zero* was published in New Rivers' Minnesota Voices Project Series in 1985. He was born in Superior, Wisconsin, where he currently lives and writes. His short stories, reviews, and essays on literature appear frequently in periodicals in Canada and the U.S.

Sharon Chmielarz is a teacher and writer. New Rivers Press published her first collection of poetry, *Different Arrangements*. She has published in a number of literary journals and has forthcoming a picture book adaptation of the "Pied Piper of Hamline" from Stemmer House in Maryland.

Helen Degen Cohen's "The Edge of the Field" (which won first place in the *Stand Magazine* competition) is part of a larger work of the same name. She was born in Poland and survived a prison camp, but has been able to write about the experience only recently. Her poems and stories appear in numerous journals. She lives near Chicago.

Victor Contoski's previous collections include *Broken Treaties* and *Names*, both published by New Rivers. His translations of Polish poets into English include Tadeusz Rozewicz and Jerzy Harasymowicz as well as Marek Baterowicz (see above). He was born and raised in the Northeast section of Minneapolis and attended the University of Minnesota and the University of Wisconsin. He currently teaches at the University of Kansas. The poems presented here come from a series based on architectural subjects.

Olivia Diamond's work has appeared in *Contact*, *Korone*, and *The Rockford Review*. She lives in Rockford, Illinois and is program chair of the Rockford Writers' Guild.

Kristine Dugas grew up in the Polish community of Milwaukee's South Side. In 1977, she was awarded a Poland's Millennium scholarship. She has lived in upstate New York and in London and currently makes her home in Columbus, Ohio.

Linda Nemec Foster lives in northern Michigan. Her poems have been published in a variety of literary magazines around the country including *Tendril*, *ACM*, and *Croton Review*. She is the recipient of a grant from the Michigan Council for the Arts and her poetry has been nominated for the Pushcart Prize. A chapbook of prose poems, *A History of the Body*, was recently published by Coffee House Press.

K.C. Frederick grew up in Detroit and currently teaches at the University of Massachusetts. His short stories have appeared in numerous publications as well as *Best American Short Stories* and *Pushcart Prize:X* (1986). "What Can You Do With A Fish?" is part of a book of stories called *On Dubois Street*.

John Guzlowski's parents were Polish peasants who suffered the war in a concentration camp in Germany. In 1951 they (and he) came to this country as DP's. He is an associate professor of English at Eastern Illinois University where he publishes *Karamu*, a little magazine. He writes that he sees himself increasingly as a Polish-American writer.

David Jauss teaches at the University of Arkansas at Little Rock and edits *Crazyhorse*. He was born in Windom, Minnesota, was raised in Montevideo, and went to school at Southwest State University in Marshall. His work has appeared in numerous journals and anthologies, including *The Iowa Review*, *Poetry Northwest*, and *Short Stories 1983: The O. Henry Awards*.

Tad Kielczewski remains something of a mystery to us. The return address he gave with the poems he sent doesn't exist and the post office keeps returning everything we send to him. He wrote in his cover letter that he is 29, has a deep interest in haiku and has been previously published in the college anthology *Rising Star* which covers the state of Wisconsin.

Edward Kleinschmidt writes that he grew up in one of the Polish communities of Winona, Minnesota. He now lives in San Francisco where he writes and teaches. His poems have appeared in numerous journals including *Poetry* and *Black Warrior Review*. Heyeck Press just published a collection of his poetry.

Linda Back McKay's family name is Traczyk. Her parents grew up in Northeast Minneapolis, and, during prohibition, her grandmother helped make ends meet by selling moonshine whiskey.

Arlene (Czekalski) Maass was born and raised in Milwaukee, "a hapless dreamer turned hippie factory worker who liked poetry." She has lived in London and Jerusalem, where her writing took a more serious turn. Her work has appeared in *Jewish Currents* and *A Blood to Remember: American Poets on the Holocaust*. She has just moved to the Chicago area after completing seminary training in Dallas.

Paul Milenski was born in 1942 into a Polish-speaking household in Adams, MA. He has worked as tobacco picker, laboratory technician, pool room manager, and teacher (grades five to graduate). In 1983, at the age of 40, he quit his job as a public school superintendent to write for publication. To date, he has sold fifty stories, won an AWP prize, and three PEN Syndicated prizes for short fiction. His story "Tickets" is anthologized in *Sudden Fiction: American Short-Short Stories*.

Linda Mizejewski teaches at the University of Pittsburgh. In 1984-85, she was a Fulbright Lecturer at the University of Iasi in Romania. She has published poetry and articles in numerous journals. Her chapbook, *The Other Woman* was the 1982 winner of the Signpost Press Poetry Competition.

Nicole Niemi is a first generation American whose maiden name, Marchewka (MA-haf-ka), means "carrot" in Polish. She has published in a number of literary journals and has worked as a storyteller. She lives in Minneapolis.

Kathryn Nocerino is the author of three books of poetry: *Wax Lips* (New Rivers, 1980), *Candles in the Daytime* (Warthog Press, 1986), and *Death of the Plankton Bar and Grill* (New Rivers, 1987). She has been a resident of the Yaddo Colony and the Ragdale Foundation. She comes from Italian and Polish bloodlines, and lives in New York City.

Ed Ochester lives in Pennsylvania. Juniper Press published a chapbook, *Weehawken Ferry* in 1985. A new book, *Changing The Name To Ochester*, is due from Carnegie-Mellon. He writes that his connection with the upper midwest dates from 1963-67 when he was a graduate student at the University of Wisconsin in Madison.

Barry Silesky lives in Chicago where he edits *ACM* magazine. His work has appeared in numerous journals such as *Abraxas*, *Grand Street*, and *North American Review*. *In the Ruins*, a chapbook of prose, won a Center Press innovative fiction prize in 1983. He and his wife are the parents of newborn twins.

Margaret Szumowski was born in Winterset, Iowa and attended the College of St. Catherine in St. Paul. Her poems have appeared in *Tendril*, *The Massachusetts Review* and *The Bilingual Review*. Her poem series "Concert at Chopin's House" reflect her husband's family history (they emigrated from Europe to

Kenosha, Wisconsin in 1952), war-time experiences, and travels with her husband and father-in-law in Poland.

Marilynne Thomas Walton grew up in the Polish farming community of Strickland, Wisconsin in Barron County. She graduated from the College of St. Catherine and worked as a librarian in St. Paul and New York City. She lives in the Como area of St. Paul with her husband and children.

Anna Wasescha is currently in graduate school at the University of Minnesota. She is an avid reader and an occasional writer. Her work has appeared in *Gallimaufry* and other publications. She lives in St. Paul.

Acknowledgments

Keith Abbott: "Raspberry Apparitions" copyright © 1984 & 1987, Keith Abbott. Reprinted by permission of the author.

Marek Baterowicz: "Three Kings," "A History Of Religion," "###(Ktoś Powiedział),"
"That Day," and "Fairy Tale," originally appeared in *Mid-America Quarterly*. Reprinted by permission of the translator. "###(Mój stary)" originally appeared in *Luna Tack*. Reprinted by permission of the translator.

Magda Bogin: "Dream Of Myself As A Fish" and "Solidarity At Dinner Time" are reprinted from the chapbook *Al Dente* Selected Poems by Danuta Vidali, copyright © 1984, To Open Press. Reprinted by permission of the author and publisher.

Sharon Chmielarz: "Marie And Ella" originally appeared in *Minnesota Monthly*. "Reading Responsively" was first published in *Slow Dancer* (UK). Reprinted by permission of the author and publishers.

Helen Degen-Cohen: "The Edge Of The Field" originally appeared in *Stand Magazine* (UK). Reprinted by permission of the author. "I Remember Coming Into Warsaw, A Child," was first published in *Spoon River Quarterly*. Reprinted by permission of the author.

Kristine Dugas: "It Is Too Cold To Change The Sheets" copyright © 1987 by Kristine Dugas. All rights reserved.

Linda Nemec Foster: "History of the Toenails" is reprinted from *A History of the Body*, Coffee House Press, copyright © 1987. Reprinted by permission of the author and publisher.

K.C. Frederick: "What Can You Do With A Fish?" originally appeared in *Shenandoah*. Reprinted by permission of the author.

Paul Milenski: "Son Of Soldier" was originally printed in *The Catholic Socialist Review*, Volume 2, Combined Numbers 1&2, and reprinted in *The Transcript*, Berkshire Writers Series, Saturday, January 10, 1987. Reprinted with permission of the author.

John Minczeski: "Columbines/Summer/1982" was originally printed in *Mr. Cogito*. Reprinted by permission of the author. "Wild Rose" is reprinted from *The Reconstruction Of Light* copyright © 1981, John Minczeski. "My Name" is reprinted from *The Spiders* copyright © 1979, John Minczeski. Reprinted by permission of the author and New Rivers Press.

Linda Mizejewski: "Keeping My Name" originally appeared in *Frontiers*, Volume 8, No. 1 (1984). Reprinted by permission of the author.

Ed Ochester: "Poem On His 44th Birthday" and "For The Margrave Of Brandenburg" are reprinted from *Weehawken Ferry*, copyright © 1985, Ed Ochester. "Cooking" is reprinted from *Miracle Mile*, copyright © 1984, Ed Ochester. "Changing The Name To Ochester" and "The Heart Of Owl Country" originally appeared in *Antioch Review*. Reprinted by permission of the author.

Barry Silesky: "Working On The Roof" was first published in *Black Warrior Review*. Reprinted by permission of the publisher. "A Day In The Country" was first published in *Ascent*. Reprinted by permission of the publisher. "The New Tenants" was first published in *Grand Street*. Reprinted by permission of the publisher.

Anna Wasescha: "The Storm" was published in *Secrets And Other Stories*, Gallimaufry 14, Gallimaufry Press, Washington, D.C., 1979. Reprinted by permission of the author and publisher.